R Thynne

Ravensdale

A Novel. Vol. 1

R Thynne

Ravensdale
A Novel. Vol. 1

ISBN/EAN: 9783337045913

Printed in Europe, USA, Canada, Australia, Japan

Cover: Foto ©Andreas Hilbeck / pixelio.de

More available books at **www.hansebooks.com**

RAVENSDALE.

A Novel.

IN THREE VOLUMES.

VOL. I.

LONDON:

SAMUEL TINSLEY, 34, SOUTHAMPTON ST., STRAND.

1873.

CONTENTS OF VOL. I.

RAVENSDALE.

CHAPTER I.

TAKEN TO TASK.

THE present century was as yet in long clothes, when I found myself, a youthful student of the law, under the legal tuition of Mr. Mark Mainmarches, of Chancery Lane, and of the Grove, Peckham.

For more time than I could be reasonably expected to call to mind, Mr. Mainmarches had filled the post of legal adviser to my father. In fact, it was no secret among us youngsters that the first and primary meeting of these two gentlemen—when they took each other's measure very sharply and very accurately—had been over those self-same "settlements" which were to confer on my parent, hitherto an Irish captain on Colonial service, a husband's right (with well-guarded restrictions, however,) over a snug country seat in Gloucestershire : in consideration of (*his* contribution to the marriage venture) an equivalent number of Irish acres, known—throughout Ireland, at least—for their excellent supply of snipe-shooting. Though I have heard my father frequently complain that " Mark Mainmarches had tied him up a deal too tight on the occasion," yet the circumstance by no means detracted from his admiration for his then adversary's legal acuteness and conscientious discharge of duty. From that hour, he had taken him (much, I suppose, on the principle which sets a thief to catch a thief) as his adviser on all points of law and property; he being unsupplied, at the time, with any person acting in that precise capacity toward him. From which, it is certainly open to inference that any the like previous appointment, in connection with our branch of the house of

Featherstone, would have been much in the nature of a sinecure. Let me add, however, that if my parent carried little with him, in the shape of property, into the concern matrimonial (barring those Irish acres), he brought a goodly stock of common sense— or shrewdness, as, without any filial irre- verence, I may fairly pronounce it; with which was joined a knack of " keeping things respectable," which, inasmuch as it is not supposed to be, at all times, characteristic of his countrymen, may have helped to earn for him the reputation of a long-headed fellow: just as we find ourselves occasionally lost in admiration of the depth and profundity of a child, which, with less tender years, might show to no such wonderful advantage at all. Not only did the Gloucestershire acres lose not in quantity—*there*, perhaps, the praise was more justly due to the aforesaid Mark Mainmarches. But, even as to quality, they always appeared well fenced and well cropped; and, if I might judge from the regularity with which tradesmen found their accounts meet, proved sufficiently remunerative for the wants of a small and quiet establishment.

The astute reader having already collected from these few preceding lines that Mr. Mainmarches had acted professionally on the female side and interests, until these interests were become identified with the aforesaid house of Featherstone, it will be admitted that, both by the maternal and paternal line, that gentleman was in all points to be regarded as "a friend of the family." When, therefore, my school and college education was adjudged to be sufficiently complete, and it became incumbent on me to embark on that further course necessary to fit me for the profession and practice of the law, the possession of such a friend and adviser as Mr. Mainmarches was considered no mean acquisition. In accordance with which view, and after some correspondence on the subject, I had been despatched to London with a letter of introduction to that gentleman, and the first quarter's portion of a moderate allowance handed to me in advance. I had now been about two years in the great metropolis; spending my time partly in Mr. Mainmarches' office, and partly in attendance on the necessary prelections and dinners. At this particular period I open my narrative, inasmuch as it brought to a close a portion of my life uninteresting to the reader, and I was now to engage in scenes and pursuits of a sufficiently different character.

Will it be thought that I once too often raise the remark, if I here observe what small and apparently contemptible events control our destinies? Either my parent took *too* moderate a view of the expenses attending a London residence, or I lacked the power necessary to the due manipulation of the funds actually at my disposal. My early quarters closed in uneasiness and apprehension, my later ones in absolute debt and despair. Yet, through the very depths of this despair, pierced a feeble ray of light, which my eye at length caught; and catching, learned to connect hopes with. A certain Mr. Jack Armstrong had passed through our office, and was now open to practise his profession. I knew his country remittances to be less regular than my own, and even smaller in amount. But, though still brief-less, he had money enough for his own wants, and even for those of his friends, if they would accept the obligation. I was less reluctant to participate in the actual source of his gains than in those gains themselves; which he was as ready to impart. He possessed, by nature, a trick of throwing off a light, trifling, but readable article, readily bought up by the conductors and owners of the few maga-zines of the day, and the greater crowd of Keepsakes, Wreaths, Garlands, Amulets, and the like flourishing productions of the period, but fated to yield the post of periodic literary supply to their less numerous contempo-raries, or, at least, our present modifications of them. My literary Mentor supplied me with subjects, hints as to style, mode of treatment ; informing me that he would sub-mit my first promising production to one of his numerous patrons. My failures were frequent, and sufficiently disappointing; in fact, they never got beyond the critical eye of Mr. Armstrong himself. But youth is the season of hope; and I still hoped and worked.

One day, as I sat on my accustomed stool, I became aware that Mr. Mainmarches was standing at the opposite side of my desk, appearing to contemplate with some interest the paper I was engaged upon; which, as happened too often of late, bore no reference to the law, or my present preparation for its practice.

Mr. Mainmarches was a short, square man, a trifle bald; with an acquiline nose, and a keen small eye, which lurked under a remarkably shaggy brow. Ordinarily, his accents were sarcastic—almost harsh; and his opinion of human nature in general (if one might judge from a stray remark now and again) far from complimentary to his species. Possibly, these qualities stood some-what in the way of anything like a close companionship between himself and his fellow-mortals. And yet, again, the dry spice of humour with which such remarks were seasoned (and by means of which they always carried the laugh *with* him) hindered the breach from assuming any very wide or irreparable proportions. In public and private life, his character was without stain; and those clients who entrusted their legal affairs to him had just cause to feel satisfied with his conscientious discharge of his duties. In a word, I have every reason to believe him an honest man—as (so he himself would have qualified such an assertion) honest men go. And this, notwithstanding the apparently contradictory fact that, while regarding, or proclaiming that he regarded, the world as an assemblage of rogues, he made no pretence to exemption in his own particular favour.

Success in life—and indifferently in all and every department and walk in life—went an immense way in Mr. Mainmarches' estimation of his neighbours; so, at least, it was his frequent pleasure to declare. If the success happened to be obtained without loss of public favour, it rose to the level of genius —the only idea of genius, I am bound to confess, which I ever discovered him to entertain. For, as to the genius which

created a "Paradise Lost" to convey away
the fee-simple thereof for some five pounds
—or that which put together the Homeric
rhapsodies to hawk about Grecian villages,
it was not of an order to obtain from that
gentleman any expression of very high com-
mendation. My father, who had converted
a somewhat uncomfortable, because penni-
less, situation in a marching regiment into
that of a squire over broad Gloucestershire
acres, always stood high in his consideration.
A fair share of which favour I had hitherto
found extended to myself.

Such was the gentleman who now stood
opposite to me, evidently waiting for a
suitable moment—to wit, when I could succeed in bringing to an end the sentence I
had been some time employed upon—to
open a conversation.

" I had a letter this morning from your
father, Master Frank. He tells me you have
been doing something in—in the literary
line."

The charge—for charge I saw it was to be
—found me prepared with no very precise

line of defence. I could have hardly appre-
hended that any very artless—and perhaps
too sanguine—confessions of mine to country
relatives would have been thus returned to
our office in the shape of a direct and un-
compromising bill of indictment, as appeared
to be but too evidently the case now. I could
only stammer forth a hope that my office
work had not been found too palpably in
arrear.

"If there's one thing," pursued that gentleman, suddenly rising from the apparently
courteous to the more unmistakably accu-
satory, and wholly heedless of my reply—
"if there's one thing which a man of my
profession shuns more than another, it's a
literary counsel, a 'junior' who dabbles in
printer's ink. I wouldn't trust one of such
cattle farther than I could throw a bull by
the horns; and if the like ever gets wind
on your father's son, your prospects at the
Bar are as good as ended."

I made haste, on the opportunity of a
pause which had every indication of being
brief, to intimate a frame of mind—possibly

the result of some disappointing experience
—not disinclined to a more exclusive devo-
tion to the business of the profession I was
adopting.

"Do you find it to pay itself?" resumed
Mr. Mainmarches, with the same apparent
heedlessness of my reply.

I was obliged to confess that I had not yet
brought my labours of a literary character
to that desirable stage.

"So!" said Mr. Mainmarches; "to think
that it should come to this with a son of
Dominick Featherstone; a poor captain, who
married an heiress out of the teeth of a whole
county! I never turned a man out of my hands
that was satisfied with anything short of a silk
gown or a serjeantship; ay, and I could count
you up judges by the half-dozen; and to find
in my old age that I should take to growing
literary hacks and Grub-street scribblers!"

Did my offence justify language of this
nature? I said to myself, no. Besides,
there were barely perceptible indications of
a less serious character, chiefly lurking about
the corners of the mouth.

However, I was now getting on my mettle, thus taunted with deteriorating the ordinary productions of Mr. Mainmarches' office ; and proceeded to state, in more measured terms, my proposed course of conduct, previously referred to.

"I have not yet taken any steps in the matter which can be pronounced decisive ; in other words, nothing of mine has been pledged to the public. I am not entirely inclined to disagree with you, sir, as to the incompatibility of the two pursuits with each other—at least, during such period as the foundations of a sound legal training are to be laid. Of course, if you make it a rule of your office, I now pass my word to that effect."

"Well, well," said Mr. Mainmarches, who seemed to pay but slight attention to these somewhat studied sentences of mine—to be talked to "like a book" was one of that gentleman's chiefest aversions—"well, well, maybe it's not as bad as we thought. At all events, if you do amend your courses, you'll not be the first young gentleman whose gait

I have stopped in that direction. Not that I would have you whistle till out of the wood. The livery of Grub Street, easily donned, is not shifted so readily as you may suppose."

Here Mr. Mainmarches, voluntarily, indulged in a pause, which, from very endurance, was becoming awkward. At length, he resumed, in a key perceptibly lighter,—

"I received an enclosure for yourself with your father's letter of this morning—backed by a request, however, that I would not transfer it to your hands until I had given you a—a (here the relaxation of the corners of the mouth was still more unmistakable) —a talk-over on the matter we have been discussing."

And handing me the note referred to, with some more words on the subject which appeared to have called forth this sudden—and suddenly subsiding—outburst, Mr. Mainmarches, with somewhat of a self-satisfied step, left me to its undisturbed perusal.

CHAPTER II.

M Y father's epistle was short, and, beyond the mere opening lines, contained no reference to the subject of the
conversation which I have just transferred to
these pages. In all probability, he deemed
the matter sufficiently well placed in the
hands of Mr. Mainmarches—and it was
preeminently my parent's habit to let well
enough alone. With this barely passing allusion, the letter, or rather note, proceeded
as follows :—

"And now, my dear Frank, I may assume
that you have already promised to confine
yourself more exclusively to your proper
study of the law. Sure am I that such promise, when passed, is made with the good
faith of a Featherstone. But, by all accounts,

the Muses are sad jades to fall into the toils of,
and keep tight grip of a man when they get
him. What say you to a little change of
scene? He who fights—but the quotation,
I make no doubt, is sufficiently familiar to a
gentleman of your literary range. Six
months would give you time to re-arrange
your mind, and to return to the pursuit of
case and precedent with a proper degree of
zest. Come here if you like—and are not
too sensitive to our bantering. But, if I
might suggest, I would say go to Ireland.
Forbye other reasons—which are as yet too
confused in my poor brain for explanation
—you will be among my own people, and
may reckon, if the times haven't changed us,
on an Irish welcome. My poor brother
Allen has often expressed a wish to see an
English Featherstone. You will find him a
trifle odd at first, but that will wear away—
he has had his troubles, and they have been
hard to bear. He has long retired from the
world, contrary to my advice expressed at
the time. But *that* should not interrupt
friendly feeling between us; and maybe it's

something of the sort that sets me putting pen to paper to you. When I wanted to make a decent show before your mother's people here, he was the first to come forward and place a few Irish acres at my disposal. To be sure, they were only unreclaimed bog, with no heavier stock than snipe: and, indeed, my brother was so candid as to have me represent as much. Anent which, I took my own counsel, and so they served their turn. And who's the worse of it? Sir Digges, my eldest brother, has, I am informed, fallen into very sad ways. He was always wild ; and, succeeding young to the headship of our house, there was little to keep him in check, barring the length of his tether — and, by all accounts, he has run that out long ago. Still, the property's entailed, and, sooner or later, must come to somebody, and life's uncertain to us all. You may call on him or not, as circumstances may dictate. I have always taken a charitable view of these things myself. At most, Castle Coote is only a short run from the Irish metro- polis. But Ravensdale, my brother Allen's

residence in the adjoining county of Wicklow, ought to be your first object. Only last
week, I had a letter from your cousin Constance—she is a daughter of my poor sister
Sophy. Sophy, as you may have heard me
mention, married Tom De Vere, who served
with me through the American campaign,
and got his billet, or bullet, at Yorktown ;
and my sister did not long survive him.
Both my eldest brother and your uncle
Allen proposed to take Sophy's child (I
was then a simple sub in a marching regiment, and hardly able to care myself), and it
was your aunt's dying request (I stood by
her bedside till the breath left her), that she
should be given to Allen. No doubt Sir
Digges' offer looked the finer ; but my sister
was firm, saying, Castle Coote was no fit
place for a young female to grow up in.
She was right ; and I carried out her com
mands to the letter, never losing sight of the
child till I placed her under Ravensdale roof.
Allen has been a father to her ever since.
She writes — I have no doubt at the sug-
gestion of your uncle—to regret that the

family is not more united at the present time;
we *were* a united family, notwithstanding
anything that may appear to the contrary
now.   I also gather from her letter (my poor
brother's vacillations of mind, to call them
by no other term, have in all probability
communicated this seeming obscurity to
portions of her letter), that the presence
of myself, or a representative of mine, would
be desirable at Ravensdale at the present
juncture.   I shouldn't be surprised if it was
your cousin's letter which has set me ram-
bling on family matters in this manner;
though I believe I told Mark to pitch into
you about the perils of Parnassus.   Maybe,
if I had you here, I could tell you more; but
I am an indifferent clerk.   After all, haven't
I told you enough?   Your uncle has turned
suspicious and secret, and may prefer to tell
his own story to having it told for him.   If
the wind sits in that quarter, sink the little
you know, and Allen may give you more
of his confidence than he has vouchsafed to
me.   Ireland, then, say I; and, if you are
of the same mind, I will drop a note to

Ravensdale to tell them to be on the look-
out for you.''

Few propositions could have been more
acceptable to me, at the time, than this one
of a trip to the sister isle. During a few
months' absence from London on my part,
Mr. Mainmarches might find time to forget
all allusions to literary hacks and Grub
Street poetasters; with which allusions,
during my suggestive presence, I was well
assured the office would repeatedly ring.
My promise, too, to refrain from all invoca-
tion of the Muses—could I be quite sure of
my power to abide by it, so long as pen,
ink, and paper strewed my daily path?
Again, futile as, I knew, would be the application for an increased allowance, whereby
to settle my more pressing accounts, while
a resident of London, I felt quite satisfied
that the first step in my proposed mission
—a mission which I was already sufficiently acquainted with the parental style
of correspondence to pronounce as lying
near to the writer's heart — would be a
clearing off of all outstanding claims. If

for no other reasons than these—and others
there were of a different character—a short
absence from the English metropolis, and
even from the more domestic Woodlands,
seemed to me highly desirable.

My other considerations may be briefly
defined as a certain natural curiosity,
springing from somewhat exceptional circumstances, to learn more of my Irish relatives. Hitherto, I knew myself only as the
lawful son of Dominick and Maria Featherstone, in the county of Gloucester—
beyond which, my knowledge of myself and
my belongings extended not, as far as
concerned the name I bore. To be sure, my
mother's people had lived and died
in the aforesaid county, and its adjoining
counties, from time out of mind, and I could
count up uncles and aunts by the score,
with cousins, male and female, to the first,
second, and more distant orders, or until
they became inextricably blended with the
surrounding families of the shire. So far,
the matter was simple enough. It was
when I turned from the English to the Irish

elements of the case that I found my information becoming vague, scanty. and incom-
plete. Not but I had long known my father
to belong to the Irish family of the Featherstones, the head of the house being represented by a certain baronet to whom reference
had just been made in the letter which now
lay before me. That my parent had served,
with some distinction, throughout the American war of independence, I was also aware—
as that, returning with his regiment, he had
then and there exchanged the sword for the
ploughshare,—a step which his marriage
at the time was mainly instrumental in
enabling him to take. Notwithstanding,
however, a certain weakness for comfortable
quarters,—which, possibly from their novelty,
I am bound to confess did distinguish my
paternal parent—I could not altogether think
that his final and absolute settlement in
England was entirely to be attributed to
the fact of having there secured his desires.
In his daily routine as a farmer, when in-
specting his wheat-fields or directing the
succession of green crops (and having put his

hand to the plough, it is but fair to state he was not the man to turn back), snatches of Irish melody have occasionally fallen from him ; and, at a somewhat tender age, my own mind was stored with much of the legendary lore of that island of saints. I could, too, call to mind the period when the question of a migration thither had been seriously debated in the family circle, in connexion with certain works of drainage, reclamation of waste lands, and improved rotation of crops ; my mother apparently being no opposing party. About that period, however, I had been despatched to one of our large public schools, and when, during a succeeding vacation, I returned to the paternal roof, all mention of main drainage, bog lands, and rotatory crops, as bearing on an Irish residence, had entirely ceased and determined. My father still continued to whistle his bits of Irish melodies, and, it might be thought, with a certain predilection for the more plaintive ones, but the subject of a removal to that country was no more discussed ; and the land

itself but rarely—never openly. Nor had
any reference been made to the members of
my father's family, until their names now
appeared—doubtless for good and sufficient
reasons—in the letter which I had just read.
Whatever might be the object of interrupting
this silence, even in so partial a manner, at
least it afforded me the opportunity of appearing before my Irish relatives not quite
ignorant of their names and circumstances.
For the rest, I trusted to the chapter of accidents—no very unusual course, I suppose,
in a young man of my years.

My preparations were soon made. In due
course, I found myself stepping on board the
small sailing vessel, dignified by the name of
packet, which then formed the chief means of
communication between the two portions of
the United Kingdom. In a few moments,
the tide allowing, with the setting sun just
resting on the horizon, we were following the
track of light still lingering on the almost
smooth surface of the Irish Channel; which
a young and somewhat fervid imagination might be permitted to regard as

marking out our way to the land of the
West.

I remained on deck until long after darkness had completely set in. Sooth to say,
my sensations were novel; and to yield to
their entire sway, I found not unpleasant for
the hour. It was the first time I had set
foot off my native soil. Then, my father's
manifest intention—plainly manifest to me,
somewhat skilled in the parental manner—to
pique my curiosity, but to leave me to my
own unassisted efforts to satisfy it; in effect,
to send me to my Irish relatives with my
finger in my mouth, as it were? And those
relatives—of what nature was to be my reception by them? With these and other
the like thoughts passing through my mind,
I was equally heedless of the growing gloom,
and the chill night wind now rising. Nor
was it until a push here, and a violent col-
lision there, informed me that I stood in the
way of the due management of the vessel,
that I betook myself to the regions below.

Making my way down "the companion,"
I found myself in the cabin, a small, close,

and dimly-lighted compartment, where such
of my fellow-passengers as had not yet be-
taken themselves to their berths, sat, in all
the various stages of somnolency. Here, a
couple blinked over a game of cribbage;
there, a gentleman, one of a small convivial
knot, and evidently loth to withdraw from
its attractions, had so far compromised matters as to indulge in a short nap, with head
and arms on the table; while, beyond him,
another, coiled up on the seat or bench, and
further provided with an ample woollen
night-cap, had wholly abandoned himself to
the influence of the drowsy god, and was
now affording audible proof that he had already accomplished all the intervening stages,
or possibly skipped them, and was far advanced into the land of dreams.

Having answered some half-dozen questions from some half-dozen persons, on the
one topic of the state of the night, and the
progress we were making; and having, in my
own proper person, during the short period
that I sat on a bench near the door, gone
through a few of the preliminary stages just

alluded to, I at length retired to my own proper compartment, and soon sank into complete oblivion.

Nor did I open my eyes until the bright morning's sun, shining through a very small round window, coupled with an unusual trampling of feet overhead, warned me that it was time to rise. In a few minutes more, I stood on deck, in time to catch a first view of the Irish coast.

CHAPTER III.

"A BEAUTIFUL sight, sir," said a somewhat deep, but by no means unpleasant, voice beside me, as my eye continued to dwell on the succession of rounded hill-top and wooded slope, forming a background, or rather enclosing amphitheatre, to the Bay of Dublin, which we were now approaching under the combined influence of bright sunshine and a genial early summer's morning. The owner of the voice I had already met on the preceding evening, both on deck and in the cabin; and, on each occasion, some trifling matter connected with the vessel had brought us into conversation. *My* impression had been decidedly favourable. It was not, therefore, without

pleasure I again recognised his tones, and,
in turning to reply to them, took a more full
glance at the speaker than the imperfect twilight had enabled me previously to do.

I beheld a portly figure, disclosing considerable broadness of chest, with corresponding breadth of shoulder. His presence
betokened a certain air of command, though
whether this was more attributable to a clear
well-set eye, or to an erectness and more
than common height of stature, I was unable
to decide. In other respects, nothing was
discernible of a military character, either
about his person or the ordinary civilian's
garb which he wore. Some forty-five, or
perhaps fifty, summers had embrowned a
frank, good-humoured set of features; and
a slight—the very slightest—flavour of the
Irish accent, just sufficient to fix the country
of its origin without launching out into the
broadness of provincialism, appeared in
keeping with the style of countenance; both
being, in a manner, racy of the soil. In his
address, the stranger had not entirely succeeded—I am not sure that he wished to

succeed—in abandoning the somewhat extreme manners of the old school : though, at
the period, their decadence was already beginning to render their use marked. This
punctiliousness, however—it extended no
further—was considerably relieved by a
certain lightness and elasticity of demeanour, which completely removed all appearance of primness. In a word, while attentive to all the minute points of courtesy
—even to the extent of those which had
already passed out of practice—a natural
buoyancy of manner communicated to this
attention all the appearance of impulse.

Having accosted me with the few words
above given, he afforded me ample opportunity for any scrutiny of him I might choose
to take, by directing his own glance to the
objects he had thus alluded to—and apparently with similar pleasure.

" The view is indeed a very fine one,"
was my reply—" seen, too, I should suppose,
under favourable circumstances ? "

" Yes ; a clear spring morning is no bad
time to view the beauties of our Dublin and

Wicklow hills; though a lowering day in midsummer—if there's no mist, and the hills look near and clear, more especially if you can get a bit of sunburst—is better, to my mind. Then some of these slopes put on their more vivid emerald and amber tints, and patches of the hill-side—it may be a native's partiality—assume an appearance nothing short of charming. Now some of my countrymen," proceeded the stranger, launching more deeply into his theme, while I continued to turn my gaze in the direction of the scene of his remarks, "are for comparing our bay with the Bay of Naples—a more injudicious attempt I cannot readily call to mind. Our bay is a fine bay, seen from here (nearer you get a view of some unsightly sandbanks), but it is not the Bay of Naples, nor very much like it."

"As this is my first step off *terra-firma*, I am by no means in a position to pronounce an opinion."

"Doubtless," said the stranger, "and very judiciously spoken; not but I have seen *that* trifling consideration no impediment to

tongues wagging, and with show of authority too. It is now a matter of some score
years since I commenced *my* travels, though,
possibly like yourself, contemplating at the
time nothing more than a cross-Channel trip
—and just so long is it since I took my last
view of those heights. It is somewhat of a
stretch to look back upon."

"It must appear so," I replied. "Travel,
then, would seem to be a serious business to
enter upon?"

"True—very true. We may not say how
long the stone will roll—or where, indeed,
it will roll to—when once it is set in motion."

"In the present instance—if I may make
so bold as to say so—back to its former
place of rest?"

"Surely—surely; that, and little more
beside. In the morning of life, we start with
large ideas of conquest—it is a kind dispen-
sation of Providence which moderates our
views with day's decline. Not, you will say,
a very original—as scarcely a very appropriate—remark to lay before a young man
whose noonday has yet to come." And, for

a moment, my companion—if I might now call him so—was silent, apparently occupied by his own thoughts.

I, too, paused, until the silence was becoming marked, and then resumed,—

" I think you spoke of the heights we are now coasting along, as the Dublin and Wicklow Hills ? "

" Of a certainty—they lie chiefly along the borders of the two counties ; though a succession of similar ranges extends through the whole of the central portions of Wicklow. I ought to know, for I was born in the thick of them ; and when the stone has rolled back there, it will be pretty nigh time to put an end to its rambles."

" I, too, am bound for the county of Wicklow, which is my reason for making the inquiry.   Possibly, you can suggest the most convenient manner for reaching my destination ?   I am informed that a coach starts daily from some part of Dublin— Henry Street, or Harry Street, if I recollect aright."

" Surely—Harry Street, it used to be in

my time, at the sign of the 'Three Travellers.'
A very regular and respectably managed
conveyance it was—and, I hope, is. But I
doubt if we shall make land in time to secure
its services to-day. The hour of starting,
unless my memory fails me, was ten o'clock
—and Miles, the name to which the worthy
whip responded, tarried neither for man
nor tide. It's now " (here the stranger applied to a large old-fashioned watch) "close
upon nine—there is a chance of the coach,
certainly—but only a chance. What say
you if we make a push for it?"

I assured my companion that my preparations were soon made. They amounted to
little more than restoring a book and some
few articles of toilet to a light travelling-bag.

" Then, there is breakfast," resumed the
stranger ; " but that, I trust, you are already
traveller enough to take against time. My
intention was to remain a night in my native
metropolis; partly, indeed, on the supposition
that our vessel would arrive too late, and
partly to renew some recollections of the
town. But if the chatter of an old traveller,

who can promise little more than an acquaintance with our common road, be not too burdensome to you, such assistance as I can render is entirely at your service, so long as our paths lie together. Ogleby is my name —Captain Ogleby, when I wore the cloth— simple Peter Ogleby in the present and future, if my countrymen (somewhat given to the weakness of 'handling' a man's name) will let me be."

Assuring Captain Ogleby that I anticipated pleasant companionship (as well as the assistance which he promised) from his offer, and giving my own name in return, I hastened below to complete my arrangements.

These were of the slightest, as I had already intimated, though somewhat delayed by an unexpected incident. This occurrence, also of itself the very slightest, dwelt in my mind longer than its nature might appear to warrant, and it is proper that I should here mention it.

While extricating my valise from a number of trunks and travelling-bags, piled rather confusedly on the deck, Captain Ogleby, in passing from one side of the vessel to the other, happened to address some observation to me (its import I entirely forget), using my name at the same time, and, as the distance rendered necessary, in a somewhat raised tone of voice. A sailor standing near, and engaged in some duty connected with the craft, appeared absolutely startled by the sound of my name thus uttered—at least, I could attribute his sudden movement to no other cause. He turned rapidly round— scanned me for a moment or two—and it was even some time before he resumed his em- ployment. The whole movement was so marked that I could not help thus connecting it with myself, and my first inference was that the man possessed some previous ac- quaintance with my father's family, most likely with the Irish portion of it. Under this impression, valise in hand—I had already secured possession of it—I drew near to him for the purpose of making some inquiry. Both build and features proclaimed him foreign ; and, presently, his accents removed all doubt. He had now resumed his employment, and, to all appearance, was undesirous of courting observation—whether this was attributable to change of mind, or a habitual reserve which had been thus involuntarily interrupted for the moment. However, my curiosity on the subject of my family having been of late on the increase, I was not disposed to let slip this opportunity—should my conjecture prove true—of adding to my slender stock of family information.

" My name appears to attract your attention ; doubtless you are acquainted with some portion of my family?"

Thus accosted, the sailor looked up from his work; though, in reply to my actual inquiry, he shook his head.

" I know not your family. You are the first Featherstone I have ever gazed face to face with, as far as my knowledge extends."

" Yet the sound of my name startled you, a moment ago?"

" True; I once heard it repeated by a passenger on board a vessel I was bound to for some years. He was in delirium, and made frequent use of the name Featherstone ; all else was incoherent. I have not since heard the name, until now. I am not long on this coast; I served chiefly in the American merchant service, and in that of my own country—Sweden. Our passenger was, to all appearances, in humble life, and his fever was the result of recent wounds. I inferred that he had been involved in the late Irish rising; that was the cause of any unwillingness you may have perceived in me to enter on the subject."

Such was the substance of the sailor's statement; of course, I omit his broken English, and his attempts—sometimes almost ineffectual—to convey his meaning to me. The man himself was not devoid of a certain rough honesty of voice and manner, and I could not doubt that he was telling me the truth, and as much of the truth as he himseli was aware of.

The near approach of the vessel to land now obliged me to hurry my preparations; for which purpose, I went below. Nor were my movements at all too quick. When I again emerged on deck, the packet had already arrived at the quay, and the shore was lined with a tumultuous assemblage of owners of jingles, noddies, whiskies, and other various vehicles—all violently gesticulating to the passengers on board. One of the most energetic of these had already caught the eye of Captain Ogleby, and I arrived in time to hear a portion of the parley which had ensued.

"Catch the Wicklow coach, your honour? —sure we can thry. Anyhow, if horseflesh can do it, man or beast won't get there before us."

"What say you, Mr. Featherstone; we can't in reason expect fairer promises?" said my new acquaintance, as I rejoined him. "Perhaps we had better close with the fellow's offer. You will find them all equally plausible, while time travels in the interim."

As I yielded acquiescence, we took our seats, and placed no further impediment in the way of our charioteer exhibiting to the full the powers of horse and man.

And, indeed, so long as there remained uninterrupted, or, at least, not very much in-

terrupted, stage, these powers were displayed
in a manner which left little to be desired,
except, perhaps, a greater feeling of security.
But on entering upon the more thickly-in-
habited portions of the city, obstructions
became more frequent; and, as we drew
still nearer to the object of our pursuit, we
were already reduced to little more than
walking pace. Indeed, on arriving at College Green, through which our route lay, this
modest rate of locomotion was seriously
threatened with further diminution. Here,
the concourse of idlers pretty nearly filled
the open space, the national university
being adequately represented by a number of
its alumni, who stood within their appropriate railings, and laid both Greek and
Latin authors under considerable contribution in passing comment on the outside
crowd of townsmen. Familiar as Dublin had
been to my ears as the "car-drivingest, tea-
drinkingest metropolis within the realm," I
was by no means prepared for such evidence
of numbers and bustle; which, however, was
partly explained by the holiday appearance

worn by all. It is not to be supposed that our Jehu bore this enforced delay with any particular exhibition of patience; so far from it, both whip and voice continued to be exercised long after the least benefit could be anticipated from either.

As might be naturally expected, the coach had already started. We arrived merely in time to see the crowd which its departure had drawn around the spot silently breaking up.

"So!" said my companion, "late—and with the further aggravation of being late by a few minutes! That last half mile we might have got over more expeditiously on foot. So terminates my first essay as guide and conductor, Mr. Featherstone."

"Better luck next time, Captain Ogleby," was my reply. "You know you gave me fair warning that the odds were against us. But, in truth, I am not sorry for fair excuse to see a little more of your good city; more especially as there would appear to be something beyond the ordinary afoot."

"Pray, sir," said my companion, address-

ing one of the by-standers, a countryman
by his garb, " might one inquire the cause of
this unusual excitement and concourse of
persons ? "

"Eh, sir," said the man, emitting a strong
northern accent, " ye'll be frae the country,
lik' mysel; but I reckoned a' folk kenned
what riding the Fringes meant ? "

" Surely," said my companion, turning to
me—" ay, surely; I forgot all about the
Fringes (more properly Franchises), notwithstanding having taken part in them,
many a time and oft."

" A solution, however, which scarcely ex-
plains itself to my English experience," was
my reply, "unless, indeed, it is something in
the nature of our Lord Mayor's show ? "

" Well, no; I doubt if your Gog and
Magog would recognise much in our trien-
nial ceremony. But we are like to be forced
spectators of the scene; and you will have
an opportunity of judging for yourself. Our
impedimenta we may consign to the care of
the coach-office; after which, we had better
betake ourselves to some place of greater

safety than this narrow and crowding thoroughfare promises to be. Movement up or
down the street is already, I should imagine,
out of the question; but, if my memory
serves me aright, a passage existed some-
where in our immediate neighbourhood, by
means of which we may gain access to more
open space—there to wait until the stream
flows by."

Suiting the action to the word—we had
already dismissed our vehicle as unfitted
for present locomotion—my fellow-traveller
applied his somewhat broad shoulders to the
compact mass which encircled us; and, after
a time, though not without strong expressions of remonstrance, the crowd exhibited
symptoms of yielding in the required direction.   Hastily following in the wake thus
temporarily opened for me, I found myself
at length shot out into a narrow alley or
court, leading at right angles to the main
thoroughfare, and, to my further relief, discovered Captain Ogleby standing beside
me.

"Hard words break no bones.   As to our

wardrobe, I suppose we appear to no worse advantage than our neighbours." And taking my arm, and conducting me through some comparatively empty streets and alleys, my companion eventually led me out on a portion of the College Green, through which our late interrupted course had lain ; where, though still prisoners, we enjoyed comparative immunity from the force of the living current, and were also in a position to receive edification from the encounters of wit continually taking place between gownsmen and townsmen.

With the ceremonial of the day, now numbered with the past, this narrative needs not to suffer interruption. On its conclusion, the concourse rapidly dispersed, and locomotion again became practicable.

" And now," said Captain Ogleby, as we proceeded from the spot, " after a hurried breakfast, and plenty of fresh air, would it not be desirable to ascertain what cheer for the inner man the town may afford us ? "

" That—with some provision for the coming night," was my reply. " As I have already made confession, I am an utter stranger to your city, and must again trust to your taking me in hand."

"Notwithstanding previous trial and result! Well, I accept the office of cicerone —not wholly without considerations of self. In truth, so much of change has already met my eye during the short period I have again become a citizen of my native metropolis, and, among all the concourse, so vainly have I sought for a familiar face, that a certain feeling of loneliness (these confessions, you will say, savour of the sod) already begins to steal over me. I shrink from the anticipation of a solitary meal, and a solitary bottle, in an inn, which, doubtless, has already experienced the change of more than one Boniface. Let me think, during the few remaining hours I have to spend here, that I am not altogether useless—*mancus* (as our young friends of the railings yonder might say) *et extinctâ corpus non utile dextrâ*. With tomorrow's light, I exchange the city for my native hill-side—pray Heaven it preserve a few familiar faces for me!"

My own short experience of travel had already discovered to me that there are few things less cheerful than to take one's solitary ease at one's inn. Further, I could readily understand how scenes once familiar, but now no longer peopled by friend and associate, would seem to intensify the feeling of isolation. Assuring Captain Ogleby, therefore, that such service, in the form of return of companionship, as I could command, was at his disposal, we proceeded in the direction of the Castle.

"If the house still stands," continued my companion, who, after this passing allusion to private feelings, now altered the tone of our conversation to one of a more general, as more lively, character, "we may eat our dinner, and smoke our pipes (I know not if you are a lover of the weed) on classic ground. When I was a somewhat younger man, and heard our Dublin chimes at midnight, the Rose Tavern was the chief resort of the wits of the day."

We had now proceeded past the Lower Castle Yard, and were ascending the hill on

which the Castle itself stands. When nearly
abreast with the Castle steps, my companion
turned down a court, which opened from the
opposite side of the street. Here, a few
minutes' walking through an exceedingly
narrow passage, with high and very old-
fashioned buildings on either side, brought
us to a large and equally old-fashioned
house. This structure exhibited numerous
symptoms of decay, and, furthermore, sufficiently indicated, by various articles of
wearing apparel, hung out by means of
poles to dry, that its former uses had been
altered to those of a somewhat different
character.

" This must be the house," said my companion, as he gazed up at it with looks indi-
cative of some perplexity ; "and yet it's *not*
the house—*tempora mutantur, et nos muta-
mur cum illis*—our young friends of the
railings have set my school-boy Latin adrift
in my head again. But, of a certainty, the
'Rose' stood here—and, indeed, this battered
front preserves somewhat of the familiar face
of an old friend about it. Howbeit, honest

Matthew Hanlon, mine host, affected a more tidy appearance; and, though he kept open house, it was not for lack of a door, as seems to be the present predicament.—Sirrah!" (here the Captain addressed a very airily-clothed young gentleman, bare-headed and bare-footed, who stood in the open doorway referred to)—"who might claim ownership here?"

"Ye may count for yourselves," said the urchin addressed, straightway proceeding to apply his fingers to aid any deficiency of our powers of calculating—"there's ould Pether Murphy mends shoes in the parlours—mother keeps a mangle in——"

"Hold! Did not one Mat Hanlon reside here—a fat man, with a nose somewhat inclined to reddish?"

The boy shook his head. "There's no Misther Hanlon near here—barrin Tim Hanlon, that keeps the New Rose, beyant, in Bridge Street."

"So!" said my companion, as he proceeded to turn from the spot, "after this second misadventure, Mr. Featherstone, I fear I must resign my commission into your hands."

"Nay, nay, Captain Ogleby, surely not—with the game now within reach ! This Tim Hanlon will, most likely, prove a son, or near relative, of the veritable Mat, removed to—to more tenantable premises—and this young gentleman will doubtless conduct us to the newer establishment, for a suitable recompense."

The urchin evincing his readiness to take part in this engagement, a few minutes' brisk walking brought us to the locality indicated by him. Here we found the Mr. Timothy Hanlon referred to—a nephew, we were not long in learning, of the former proprietor of the " Rose," who intimated his readiness to take us in hand, and attend to our wants.

CHAPTER IV.

A TÉTE-À-TÉTE.

AFTER we had concluded our meal, and, at my companion's solicitation, I had been induced to make trial, with him, of the national beverage—to wit, some whiskey punch, smoking hot in tumblers—Captain Ogleby lit his pipe, and threw himself back in his chair; evincing, on the whole, a more marked disposition than I had yet seen to relax from the somewhat ceremonious manners of the old school, to which I have already drawn the reader's attention as characterising his earlier address.

"Perhaps," proceeded he, after he had brought his pipe into full working order by a few preliminary whiffs—"perhaps, had my tastes been more with the fashions of the

day, I should have urged claret; but with so
few familiar faces to meet (still harping on
the string, Mr. Featherstone), I could ill
dispense with an old friend."

" The potation surely needs no apology,"
replied I, a preliminary mouthful having
assured me that the mixture—one sufficiently
novel to English tastes at the period—was
not altogether unpalatable.

" Doubtless; and yet, Mr. Landlord,"
(Mr. Hanlon had lingered for a few moments
in the room,) "your worthy uncle kept an odd
drop by him, which smacked more of the
mountain heath and less of the exciseman's
supervision?"

Mr. Hanlon's countenance, it appeared to
me, was not entirely free from alarm as he
turned to respond to these words.

" My uncle, gentlemen, was a rash man
when the sup was in him; and lost, at times,
by over-confidence in chance customers."

" Surely—surely," said my companion;
" I have heard as much; more's the pity.
But I have served your uncle a turn ere this,
young man; at a time when Peter Ogleby,

of Tinnaheely Lodge, was no stranger to the
metropolis, and was even less likely to pass
for a gauger. I doubt not you have heard
the name from your relative?"

But a moment's reflection and scrutiny
seemed already to have convinced Mr. Hanlon of his error, even before the foregoing
words had been quite spoken. He now
hastened to apologise for his momentary
doubts. "No one was likely to take an
Ogleby for a gauger; but folks living under
the eye of the Castle had need to be cautious.
If his uncle was alive, it's the best in the
house he'd hasten to lay before anyone that
belonged to Tinnaheely."

"Ay, ay; I daresay," replied my companion; "but as my young friend here
confesses to an objection to ghostly visitations—forbye, having no particular desire on
my own part——"

A faint corruscation twinkled for a moment
in the eye of Mr. Hanlon, as, crossing over
the floor, and opening a press which I had
not hitherto perceived, he drew therefrom a
stone-coloured jar. Placing this on the table,

he added, "if it was my uncle himself, gentlemen (the Lord betune us and harm), he
couldn't set before you better than that."
Then, throwing a few additional sods of
native peat on the fire (for though summer
was now advancing, the evenings were as yet
chilly), and having shifted the position of the
kettle on the hob, *more cauponum*, without
any assignable cause—he finally closed the
door behind him, and left us to ourselves.

"Ay, ay," said my companion, whose nose
was already applied to the place where the
cork had previously been, "*that* smacks of the
mountain-side and the peat smoke; I could
almost fancy I was sitting by my own turf fire
in old Tinnaheely Lodge—please the pigs! I
will, before nightfall to-morrow, *dum superest
Lachesi quod torqueat:* confound those college
lads! I am as full of Latin—and, it may be,
as doubtful Latin—as a young gentleman
going up for his entrance examination. And
now, my young friend, when you have tossed
off that drop of Parliament in your glass, let
me recommend you to try your hand at a
small potation of the *poteen*."

" My experience, I fear, scarcely reaches to the difference between the two mixtures— are they not both the product of the barley- corn ? "

"Of a verity," said my companion ; " the one manufactured by the licensed, or author- ised distiller, whence its title, Parliamentary, or legal ; the other the result of illicit dis- tillation, deriving its peculiar properties from the mountain stream and peat fire, which are essential to its due manufacture. When we get you down among our native glens (I ex- pect an early visit, Mr. Feathertone, now that we are to be near neighbours — a bachelor's establishment—indeed, for some years now an old maid's, with nothing, however, more formidable in the shape of womankind than my sister),—you shall examine the whole process for yourself, and taste the liquor as it comes from the worm, hot and strong : how- beit, for ordinary tipple, your novice may essay it qualified with a little sugar and water. And now that we are alone, I am sorely tempted to infringe on the ordinary rules of politeness—for which, were I a few potations deeper in the night, I might plead the potency of our landlord's mountain dew."

" I was under the pleasing belief," was my reply, though not without some curiosity as to the drift of my companion's latter words, " that I had already got beyond those outworks of rigid etiquette with Captain Ogleby ? "

" Faith ! the plea (neatly put, and readily conceded) sounds better than the poteen, and I am more inclined to avail myself of it, in propounding a question which has been playing sad pranks with my poor wits this whole day — in fact, ever since we interchanged names this morning on the deck of the packet. Was there not—to plunge at once into the matter—a Sir Percy Featherstone ? I can bring to my mind (it's as much as I can do) a very old man of that name about Dublin town."

" Yes ; such an individual, I am informed, there certainly was—a member (though I believe not a very near one) of my father's family. Sir Digges Featherstone, who eventually succeeded to the title, is the present head of the family, and my father's eldest brother."

"Ah! I recollect Sir Digges, as it were yesterday; not indeed as a companion, for I was then but a bit of a boy, when your uncle set the laws of fashion to Bachelor's Walk and Merrion Square. He was then plain Digges Featherstone, though waiting (and not without some need, the town said—these were awful times of fast living, Mr. Featherstone) for Castle Coote. So, so—I am getting hold of the end of the skein. But was there not another brother, learned in the law? Egad! it might be your father?"

"No, no," said I, scarcely refraining from a smile at the idea of my respected parent in a horse-hair wig, and armed with a blue bag; "my father is a country squire, and was a soldier, with all a soldier's suspicions of the quirks and quicksands of the law. Doubtless, you refer to another of the brothers, intermediate between my father and Sir Digges, who, as I have heard, made somewhat of a name for himself at the Irish Bar, before he retired into private life. My present visit to Ireland is intended for him."

" Ay—surely," said my companion, "that will be the man. He was nearer to my own age, though a shade older. The circumstance is somewhat fresher to my mind in consequence of a letter or two which I received, when abroad, from my sister. We were just then engaged in some small law matters, which—being tied to my post—I was obliged to let my sister fight out by herself. I recollect she wrote to me that Allen Featherstone—ay, Allen was certainly the name—was then the most able advocate at the Irish Bar, and ought to be retained for our case."

" I have no doubt it will prove to be the same; Allen is certainly my uncle's name—of Ravensdale House; but *that*, I believe, is a comparatively recent title; the place, I think, was formerly known by a strictly Irish appellation."

" It must have been so. I can call to mind no so-named locality," said my companion, shaking his head after some time apparently spent in reflection. "There was, to be sure, Glan-na-fiac, or the Valley of the Ravens, a few miles from Ballybay; of which we may take Ravensdale as a near translation. The county is full of such natural ravines; there is a Glan-na-mole, or Valley of the Thrushes, beside my own place."

"Ballybay is certainly the nearest town or village, according to my instructions."

For a moment my companion was silent, apparently following out the thread of some by-gone reminiscences. Presently, he resumed :—

"You never heard, then (plague take the matter!—your pardon, Mr. Featherstone; it seems to be getting faster grip of me)—you never heard the reason for your uncle's retirement from his profession?"

"No; I confess I never heard any cause assigned. Indeed, about the time, my schooling removed me from my father's house; and, my college course succeeding, I was almost entirely a stranger to the domestic roof; as, also, to much of the family history."

"It's on my mind; and, doubtless, I shall be able to trace it out. Yes; it's like a dream to me that I did hear some account of the matter."

Not feeling quite certain whether my companion addressed these words to me, or was merely giving expression to his own train of thought—the latter supposition appeared to me the more probable—I made no attempt to reply. In truth, much as my curiosity had been of late aroused to learn if any mystery did really hang over the house of Ravensdale, I shrank from pushing my inquiries, or even evincing my ignorance, before a comparative stranger. "A few days' patience," thought I, "an d I shall know all; if, indeed, anything is to be known."

But already my com panion—who ordinarily was far from betraying any want of delicacy—had perceived my embarrassment, if I might apply so strong a word to the feeling which had thus momentarily exercised influence over me. He now broke in :—

"But enough on *your* side, Mr. Featherstone. Change, long absence from home,
and a general smattering of European affairs,
have all lent their aid to mix up and
confound facts and occurrences in my poor
brain; and, in all probability, I have been
associating your worthy uncle in my mind
with some Continental gossip, or diplomatic
secret. It is now time I should endeavour
to balance the account (more especially as I
am to regard you as our promised guest) by
informing you who and what are the persons
you are to meet at Tinnaheely Lodge—when
you honour its roof. To be brief—they
comprise myself and my sister, an old
bachelor and an old maid, who (proclaim it
not, ye discreet walls!) has, I believe, a
trifle the start of me in respect of years. If
your curiosity extends further to learn how I
became a sojourner in strange lands, the
record is at your service. While I was up
in town here attending to my college studies
(I will spare poor Tabby's feelings, and not
say how long ago) my sister managed our
few acres, and kept matters together.

When I returned, with 'Bachelor of Arts' tacked to my name, I lacked the heart— you may add the inclination, if you wish—to take the control out of her hands. The soil was poor—one of those light upland strips, a cross between a mountain and moorland, which much of the central portions of Wicklow and Wexford consist of; with enough of rocks and glens, brawling stream and thundering waterfall to furnish out a decent page in the guide-books, but ever crying to the farmer, 'Give, give,' instead of 'Take, take;' and I possessed not the needful capital to satisfy its hungry propensities. Cheese-paring, if you will have observed, Mr. Featherstone, is distinctly a female passion. A man may be a miser or a spendthrift— one extreme or the other; but it is only a woman who can pinch and squeeze under a less reward than dying a half million or so above or below zero. We lack 'management' —when we acquire it, it is with loss of ease and temper. We chafe under the petty contrivances and small shifts which the womankind exalt into that virtue which is to be its own recompense; in a word, I take it that you or I would sit at the head of a stingy household with as ill a grace as we'd move in petticoats, or set off the last new style of bonnet. Had I made the attempt to carry on Tinnaheely Farm, I should, most probably, have impaired a naturally tolerable peace of mind, and made a mess of the concern. My sister, on the contrary, preserved her placidity, and exhibited a clear balance-sheet at the end of each year; and—if the truth must be told—has, ere this, come to my assistance under a pinch. Well, that's over now; for, as I said, I am speaking of a consideration of twenty years ago ; and, after debating over the matter in my own mind, I determined to leave farming to Tabby, who had proved her right to it, and to seek fortune by some less uncongenial road. Most roads, then, lead to London—to attempt but a poor parody on the older dictum ; though a young man with no particular talent, and a purse all as one as empty, set a hard fight before him twenty years ago in your capital, Mr. Featherstone. I made effort to keep

head above water by the exercise of my pen;
I might have done better at it had I felt able
to attach myself to any one of the more
powerful political parties which then held the
chief patronage in their hands. But, unfor-
tunately—like most young men hot from the
universities—I was highly tinged with the
' Liberalism' just struggling into light over
Europe. Your neighbours, the French,
shelved Liberalism for the day—and my pen
was idle. A poor commission in a marching
regiment was all my friends—patrons, if you
like, Mr. Featherstone—could place at my
disposal. Of course, I took it—anything
was better than going back to Tinnaheely,
with my finger in my mouth. As fortune
would have it, a succession of active service
enabled me to make it somewhat more remunerative than I could have originally
expected; that is, I have brought back
enough to put the farm under a proper
system of cultivation, and to allow my sister
—and those under her rod—a little ease
from pinching and toil. There! you have
the brief chronicle of Peter Ogleby, ex-

journalist, ex-captain, and now farmer ex-
pectant. Confess to a certain feeling of disappointment. Your first specimen of an
Irishman on his native soil should carry
more prominently the features of his country.
I lack the imperial ideas of your own
countrymen—and, mayhap, talk too reasonably for an aboriginal; but, in truth,
travel has given me somewhat of a cosmo-
politan turn. Take me for a poor specimen
of the Travelled Irishman, and suspend your
final judgment until you meet the real unsophisticated native."

"Pray Heaven I fall into as safe hands,
Captain Ogleby!"

"Well, well—keep your opinions to yourself about the late Union—unless you can
abuse it; and practice yourself a little more
perfectly in the poteen. There are bounds
to my countryman's patience, and if you
refuse to wax mellow at his bidding, I may
not answer for the consequences. But, be it
known to you, for politico-potatory discussions
(and their matutinal results) you are just now
going somewhat out of the Irish world, in

your present trip to Wicklow. A little more toward the west of the Shannon, or even in this metropolis itself, were your stay to be prolonged, I would recommend the addition of a brace of hair-triggers to your qualifications as an Irish tourist. But, some five years ago, you will bear in mind, the scourge of war swept over that and the adjoining county——"

"You allude, of course, to the rebellion immediately preceding the Union ? "

" The same; and the inhabitants, I suspect, have had enough of fighting for some time to come ? "

" My relatives (pardon the interruption)— my Irish relatives, I believe, bear a loyal name?"

" Preeminently so. Whatever causes may have influenced—rather, I should say (my poor head rambles at times)—any disloyal or unconstitutional act is the very last I should expect to hear told of a Featherstone of *my* day—I may not of course speak of the young fry; and, indeed, it's like a dream to me—not that *that* has any connexion—tush !

I wander—old Sir Percy was an independent supporter of the Irish Administration—much looked to for his influence with the peasantry, which he always applied to conciliatory purposes—and your uncles hold, or held, commissions in the peace. Though absent from Ireland, my quondam connection with the press kept me more or less *au courant* with these matters;—but where was I?"

"You spoke of the consequences of the Irish rebellion."

"Ay; you will find your neighbours, therefore, lying under a peaceful reaction. May we hope—I have borne the King's cloth, Mr. Featherstone—that the whirlwind has cleared the political atmosphere?—or are action and reaction still further to repeat themselves? But our lights burn low; and you will not be prevailed upon to trust our mountain dew further than a stranger's shake of the hand. What say you? Will you enter on your poteen practice, or are you for making trial of our landlord's sleeping arrangements?"

I was not sorry to avail myself of the choice, and at once elected for bed. In truth, the hurry and bustle of the day were beginning to tell upon me, leaving me under slight apprehension that strange quarters and new scenes would interfere with my slumbers. Nor did the event deceive me; for my head was scarcely on the pillow when I had already sunk into unconsciousness of all around me.

CHAPTER V.

THE sleep into which I had fallen remained unbroken, until a light tap at my bedroom door aroused me. Starting up, I was surprised to find a warm, bright sun streaming into my room: in another moment, my companion of the preceding day stood at my bedside, fully dressed, shaved, and apparently equipped for his day's journey.

"Good gracious! Captain Ogleby," I hurriedly exclaimed; "it is not possible I have so completely overslept myself! Is there danger, then, of again missing the Wicklow coach?"

"No, no," replied he, laughing. "We have time by the forelock to-day; and the apology has to come entirely from me. By nature, or habit—it may be both—I rise early; and this morning, after a vain attempt to beguile the time by strolling through dark passages and cheerless rooms, an uncontrollable desire to anticipate our pre-agreed mode of conveyance has got hold of me. I am come, therefore, to say good-bye—or ———''

" Or what, Captain Ogleby?"

" Faith, to ask you to make a similar start of it yourself. I know—or should know—a short path across the Dublin Mountains, which ought to be nothing to your young legs; the difference in point of expedition will be met by our earlier start; our ways do not diverge until I have placed you almost within sight of your destination. I am sending on a few of my own belongings by coach, and I can insure yours being delivered in safety."

" I should like the trip of all things."

" Your hand on it, then. In sooth, I so far anticipated the success of my proposition as to order a half-awake waiter, whom I stumbled over, to lay a knife and fork for you. He is now engaged in the preparation of a pan of hot chops; for, though the journey may be accomplished under some half-score of miles, they are Irish miles, and up-hill; and I would not have you attempt them on an insufficient foundation."

In a short time, my toilet was completed, and I rejoined Captain Ogleby in the coffee-room; which, owing to the earliness of the hour, we had to ourselves. During the few intervening moments, he had apparently been by no means idle. A very appetising little meal now awaited us, to which the worthy Captain pointed with a mingled expression of pride and affection.

"I take no small credit to myself, Mr. Featherstone, for my performances of the morning. One of the housemaids found me in despair over what refused to be a fire, and, I confess, took *that* task out of my hands; but the rest I may say I had a chief share in preparing—and I have just directed our luggage to follow by coach. Five-and-twenty minutes, or say the even half-hour, for breakfast, and it must be a fast whip will come up with us on this side of the Sugar-loaf Mountain."

"Excellently done! Mr. Featherstone—
with a minute or two to spare," said my
companion, as I rose from the breakfast-
table within the specified time; "and now
our little bill (reasonable enough, I must confess) is settled—no words: you shall strike
an even balance when we get you at the
Lodge—and nothing remains to delay our
start."

Half-an-hour's walking through a portion
of the town, evidently once important, but
already exhibiting signs of decline, brought
us out on the Green of Harold's Cross. Here,
the land—rising, at first, by gentle and
almost imperceptible gradation, and then
more abruptly to the summit of the Dublin
range—lay expanded before us, and wholly
visible.

For some time, our way through this
ascending space—intimately associated with
the tale I am about to unfold—lay along
devious winding roads and cross-roads, over-
shadowed by large trees, now burst into
green leaf. Occasional breaks in the ranks
of these exhibited to much advantage the

mountain flanks on one side rising above us, and, on the other, the valley of the Liffey with the city we had just left, now sinking lower and lower beneath us at every advance we made. Ever and anon, we passed some quaint old-fashioned road-side house, with its high enclosing walls, closely-barred gate, and other signs and symptoms of a silent and mysterious isolation, which might have made the fortune of a Minerva-press romance-writer of the period.

A similar half-hour's walking had already brought us to the village of Rathfarnham; a little beyond which we fairly counted ourselves as actually on the flanks of the hilly range. My companion, however, made no attempt to breast the mountain side, but skirting along, and amid, its lower portions, followed some apparently well-remembered path, for we had now completely abandoned the road. As for our conversation, it could not be fairly described as flagging. It might be that each turn of the way, each new combination of view, was recalling in my fellow-traveller associations which, under less rigid

rules of etiquette than those that guided him,
would have reduced him to silent reflection ;
or—and the supposition more than once
forced itself upon me—a guarded avoidance
of the subject of my family, even to the ex-
clusion of topics which might indirectly lead
to it, was producing in him a hesitation and
perplexity which, at times, did take the form
of silence, and, at best, of desultory conversation.

With myself, youth—unencumbered by
cares of any very considerable magnitude—
opposed no barriers to the inspiriting influence of the pure mountain air—the fragrant
odour from heath-bell, furze, and a various
hill-side flora which·breathed around—and
the delightful prospect growing more extended at every step we surmounted. Here,
we passed over a rising knoll sacred to the
purple heath, or bright yellow furze, alone.
Anon, we came upon a green ocean of fern,
through which the nut-brown, but transpa-
rent, streamlet brawled, leaping from rock
to rock, and forming here and there some
deeper pool ; presently, our path conducted

us through one of those woodland strips, where the young fir and its various cone-bearing brethren loaded the air with their aromatic fragrance, and the native blue-bell, in close and endless profusion, formed a carpet for the foot. Such was my first acquaintance with the beauties of the Dublin Mountains—no unsubstantial creation of the imagination.

We had now proceeded some miles along the flanks of the range, and having again struck the road, were approaching a somewhat singular natural feature. The mountain-side, which we had now more fairly directed our faces toward, bore the appearence of having been cleft by a deep natural chasm or cut, extending quite through the hill; and as we entered upon " the Pass," a shelving naked bank rose almost precipitously on each side of us, consisting solely of large granite blocks, heaped together in the wildest confusion, and apparently arrested, at some remote period, in their race to fill up the rent which had been caused. Through this our way wound, several blocks of stone, of the same size, having been rolled to the road-side to make room for the ordinary traffic.

" This," said my companion, "is called the Scalp—we now stand on the borders of the two counties. Here we part; your way lies somewhat to the left. It is now (here Captain Ogleby consulted his watch) close upon noon. By following the path on which we stand, you should reach Ballybay a little on the other side of the hour. The mountain mist is your only peril—and I doubt not (with a glance to windward, and toward the summits of the chief peaks) but it will be strong up among the hills before day declines. With moderate walking, however, you should be long clear of this high table-land, and, in fact, close on Ballybay, before Douce, or the Keeper (properly, the Kippure Mountain, to our right here) puts on his cap. My way lies farther, and more to the right. I would ask for your companionship through a somewhat lonely tract of country, were it not that the request might seem to outrage all propriety, in the face of your present, and more pressing, visit to your relatives. When you report the claims of kindred as complied with, I must then ask you to bear the Lodge and its inhabitants in mind."

For the first time, it now occurred to me that I had been somewhat wanting in my own offers of hospitality—so far, at least, as the close relationship existing between myself and the inmates of Ravensdale House might warrant me in making them. This, in all probability, was now the more conspicuously brought before my mind on mention of the much farther distance which yet lay between my companion and the termination of *his* journey. I, therefore, replied—though not, perhaps, wholly without some hesitation, arising from my very slight acquaintance with the circumstances and peculiarities—if they had any of note—of the persons I was about to visit.

" I could not, I fear, with any regard to good manners, delay much longer my appearance at Ravensdale House. My father spoke of writing — in any case, my arrival is expected about this time.

Possibly, however, Captain Ogleby lies under no similar necessity? The visit is my first to my Irish relatives ; but I do not think I take too much upon myself, even setting aside all considerations of Irish hospitality, in assuring a welcome from my uncle."

" No, no, my young friend—at least, not now. Old maids are apt to grow fidgety (forbye, it's in the family), and if my appearance were delayed much beyond the arrival of the Dublin coach, Heaven knows what accidents by flood and field (by which you must understand the English packet and the mountain mist) might fill my sister's head ! When you have fulfilled a kinsman's duties, and paid your own promised visit to the Lodge, you shall find me a more ready guest at the Valley of the Ravens. As for the journey now before me, I shall be guided by circumstances. If my legs betray indications of failing me, I shall allow myself to be picked up by the coach. In any case, I am pretty sure of ' a lift ' from some returning Wicklow or Gorey farmer."

And so saying, with a friendly shake of

the hand, Captain Ogleby turned from the spot; and, in a few moments more, his portly form was completely hidden from view by the foliage, and devious nature of the path down which he was descending.

CHAPTER VI.

A HILL-SIDE ADVENTURE.

M Y own path lay before me, pretty accurately defined; and with another
glance at the one or two " bearings " which
Captain Ogleby had desired me to use as
additional safeguards, I struck into it.

I had advanced, however, but a little way,
when the noise of a vehicle in rapid motion
struck on my ears. In a few moments more,
a turn of the path disclosed the high road
(which I had recently abandoned), pursuing
its winding course almost under me, while
on it a small and light carriage, drawn by
two horses, was approaching with great
rapidity the singular cleft in the mountain,
where I had so lately parted from my companion. From the appearance and move-

ment of the animals, I could have little doubt that they were in actual and uncontrolled flight, though, as they were now breasting, or at least partially breasting, the hill-side, their motion was somewhat retarded by that circumstance, and I trembled to think what fearful acceleration of speed the vehicle might receive when it had reached the Scalp, and the road thence lay entirely down hill. Nor will the reader consider my expressions of feeling exaggerated when I inform him that the carriage, now almost under me, contained the single figure of a young and graceful girl, while the reins had escaped from the vehicle so as to be wholly irrecoverable by her.

The descent to the road, though steep, was sufficiently protected by underwood, of which I could have availed myself. And there was yet time for me, had my efforts taken this course, to stand before the runaway horses. I perceived, however, that the side of the road opposite to that over which I stood was wholly unprotected, forming, in fact, the shelving slope of the hill round which the road itself was winding; nor could I doubt that the least deviation of the horses, so likely to occur in any efforts I might make to stop them, would have inevitably sent steeds, carriage, and its fair occupant to the bottom of the deep and dark valley which lay below. On the other hand, there was yet time for me to regain the Scalp, where both sides of the road were fully protected by high cliffs. The difference in distance, to me and the carriage, was very greatly in my favour, when measured against the winding road ; while, as my path had been somewhat ascending, I had now the further advantage of an incline to run down ; that is to say, while my course lay down the *chord* of an arc, the carriage would be obliged to traverse that arc itself.

To deliberate was to lose every hope of affording assistance, and scarcely had my eye taken in the whole scene when I was again hurrying along the way which I had so lately trod. The carriage was now wholly hidden from sight, though the sound informed me it was still in rapid motion ;

and with this sound in my ears, I re-entered the Pass, and—time still permitting—proceeded hastily up it, in order that the horses might get well into the defile before they obtained view of me. Scarcely had I done so when the animals appeared at the entrance. They were now on level, if not actually descending ground, and their acceleration of speed was at once apparent. Quickly retiring behind one of the large boulders, or blocks of stone, which stood by the road-side, within a few feet of which the carriage must pass, I awaited its approach. In a moment, steeds and carriage were upon me. Heedless of the cloud of mingled dust and spray, I fixed my eye on the bridle-rein which depended from the flake-covered bit, and was so fortunate as to find it firmly in my grasp. On bit and bridle, I could not but feel, now hung, in no small measure, the fate of us all ; had either given way, steeds and carriage must have passed over me, and the horses, driven desperate by my sudden and unexpected apparition, would have plunged madly down the mountain side.

But both were good, and well sustained the pressure and weight of my body, now, of necessity, thrown upon them. I was carried several yards in advance, but by the time the vehicle had lost its *vis momenti* we all stood panting on the road-side in the midst of the Pass—the horses fairly on their haunches, I, hatless, and gazing on an exceedingly beautiful young girl, who had successfully maintained her position in the carriage.

I was about to address some words of inquiry, as well as I was able, to this young lady, when a loud voice on the road—partly accosting myself, and partly my new companion—drew my attention.

" Splendidly done ! my dear young friend. Not hurt, Lucy ?—God be praised ! Splendidly done, indeed, my dear sir. I saw you on the height over the road, and was apprehensive you should endeavour to stop the carriage there—shouted with all my might—suppose I might as reasonably have attempted to direct some one in the moon. Excellent thought of you to make for the

Scalp!—saw your purpose, and hurried on after you."

The stranger, who now restored to me my hat, and grasped me most cordially by the hand, was a tall elderly man, of unmistakeably dignified presence. As he stood by the young lady for the purpose of further assuring himself of her perfect safety, I could have no doubt that I gazed on father and daughter. Words the fair occupant of the carriage had none for me just at present— but if a glistening eye, and a set of features charmingly struggling between a natural bashfulness and a desire to express frank gratefulness, could be taken as their substitute, I was already rewarded. After a moment spent in mutual congratulations, the elderly gentleman again turned toward me. Now that first excitement had in some measure subsided, I could perceive that his features and bearing were expressive of a certain grave seriousness, apparently the result of habitual exercise ; to which, rather than to any natural gift of outward form, was doubtless attributable that dignity of demeanour just alluded to; deprived of this, the stranger before me would have still been a benevolent-looking man, but without any particular mark of dignity.

"I got down to adjust a trace—unluckily without a firm hold of the reins—extremely careless on my part : we must not, my love, come to town without attendance again. Well, well, all's well that ends well. But get into the carriage—plenty of room ; doubtless you are for town ? No fear of the cattle—they seem quiet enough now."

"I have just come from Dublin," I replied, glancing, not without regret, at the seat which the fair Lucy herself was setting aside for me on this intimation from her father.

"Ah! and I must be at Court by twelve. Go you far into the county Wicklow ?—surely we are not to part thus ! Lucy, my love, what is to be done? If you should happen to be in the neighbourhood of St. Kevin's, you might relieve us somewhat of our load. Perhaps you will bear the address in mind ? My daughter, Miss Warden, whom you have so gallantly rescued—possibly the name of John Warden, that which I have previously borne, is not unfamiliar to your ears?"

My knowledge of Irish affairs, short as it was, enabled me to find that I was now in conversation with a dignitary of the Irish Judicial Bench, whose public services and acknowledged reputation for wisdom and moderation in the late most critical times, had procured his recent elevation to the peerage, under the title of Lord Killgrove.

"I am on my way to Ravensdale House, my lord," I replied, "to visit my relatives."

"Ah! a relative of my old friend, Allen Featherstone — not his son, surely? — not Leslie Featherstone?" — and Lord Killgrove's countenance for a moment grew almost severe. "But no, no; I see you must be at least three or four years younger —though a Featherstone; yes, most certainly a Featherstone."

"I am a nephew of Mr. Allen Featherstone, just come over from England for the first time."

"Yes, yes; I might have known. Poor fellow! poor fellow! Young man—my dear young friend, be wise; be prudent: we live in difficult times, apt to mislead the young and generous mind. Will you give my kind remembrance to my very esteemed friend, your uncle? We were rivals—friendly rivals, for many years, at the Bar. Egad! I might be plain John Warden still, had Allen Featherstone continued the contest. Well, well; I did my utmost to commit professional suicide by stoutly advising him against the course he pursued; but it was not to be. Lucy, my love, will you not bid good-bye to our friend, Mr. Featherstone? Plenty of shooting and fishing about St. Kevin's, if they lie in your way."

Thus called upon, the fair Lucy blushed—hesitated—and, with a still glistening eye, held forth a small hand, which clasped—sensibly clasped—mine for a moment; and, in a few moments more, I was, for the second time, standing alone in the mountain Pass.

Thus, anon thinking over my unexpected adventure, and now busied in anticipations of my visit to the Valley of the Ravens, I struck into the path pointed out to me by Captain Ogleby—and, at length, made a fair start of it.

CHAPTER VII

FOR some time, the thick underwood and the gently undulating character of the ground afforded a pleasing contrast to the barren and abrupt ruggedness of the Scalp. Presently, however, these signs disappeared, and I found myself entering upon an apparently unproductive district, most sparingly interspersed with a few wretched cabins, or hovels, of the peasantry. Annexed to each of these latter was a small and most miserable-looking patch of cultivation—if, indeed, it deserved the name, appearing very little better than the surrounding common. Gradually, too, even these vestiges of human habitation became more rare. At length, my course lay through an elevated, uninhabited tract of table-land, composed of the

real Irish peat, or bog, thinly clothed with
heath and furze—not without a marshy spot
here and there. This would have afforded
me but slight concern, as—having previously
learned that Ravensdale House lay in a comparatively fertile district—I was in momentary
expectation of seeing before me a drier and
more inviting portion of country. But a new
and far greater source of uneasiness was now
rapidly disclosing itself. The sun, which
had hitherto appeared in unclouded majesty
overhead, was becoming more and more
obscured, and a dense fine vapour, borne on
the wings of a light breeze, was descending
down the sides of the higher headlands, and
threatening every moment to envelope the
entire scene in complete obscurity. The
Sugar-loaf and one or two other heights
loomed shapeless, and more gigantic still,
for a while—and then were entirely blotted
out. Nor could I say how long the path, or
half-formed road, on which I trod would be
allowed to preserve sufficient indications to
enable me to distinguish it from the surrounding tract. To lose one's way, or

become benighted, in this inhospitable waste, afforded a prospect by no means cheering, and, insensibly, I continued to quicken my pace, notwithstanding all peril of pitfall and precipice. The curlew uttered his singularly lone and melancholy cry as he rose on the wing at my approach. The snipe started from his marshy bed, and cleaving the thick dull air in his peculiar zigzag movement, was soon lost to sight in the impenetrable gloom which hung around. The lapwing, indeed, idly flapped about my head for some time longer; but she too, rightly inferring that her nest was free from detection on such a day, grew less frequent in her gyrations, and eventually vanished behind the same dark curtain. At length, the sun—shorn of every beam, and not without difficulty distinguishable as to his position in the heavens—was the one sole object of nature, animate or inanimate, which remained visible—and the mountain mist had fairly closed around me.

How long I had adhered to the path, I was unable to judge ; that I was no longer upon it, appeared to admit of little doubt. The ground

on which I now trod was entirely composed
of furze, peat, and a very much thicker crop
of heath, with occasional shallow pools, or
" flashes " of water. A certain cold, chilling
atmosphere, too, furnished an additional
reason for my supposing that I was in the
midst of a large tract of bog land. The surface
of the ground had now become somewhat
more level, and, as I continued to proceed, the
mist, which had hitherto lain close on the soil
—mingling, indeed, with the heather-bell and
bog lichens—now began to exhibit signs of
rising to a higher altitude above the surface.

Partially encouraging as these latter symptoms might appear—indicating, at least, that
I had reached a comparatively lower and
more level tract of country—they were, however, wholly overbalanced by another circumstance, which I could not regard without a
certain feeling of uneasiness; if my manhood
would not allow me to say of alarm. I was
unable to resist the impression that for some
time now (on the most moderate calculation,
I must have been walking for three, or,
perhaps, four hours, since I had parted from

my companion of the morning) I was no longer alone in my journey. It is true that I heard nothing, and the little I saw failed, on closer inspection, to give strength to any such supposition. Yet when I had again resumed my course after every such inspection, and had succeeded in turning my thoughts to other and more distant objects, something very like a human head, enveloped in a cap, appeared to me, ever and anon, to rise above some acclivity close by, and then sink out of sight again; and, more than once, I could not divest myself of the feeling that the barrel of a gun was discernible amid a neighbouring furze-bush. I hastened to the acclivity, indeed; but the rising mist showed me nothing visible in the human form. I struck the furze-bush with my stick, but it only swayed mournfully to and fro in the vapour-laden air. That I could *hear* nothing, was of little account toward assuring me; the springy nature of the soil would have permitted even a large body of men to pass noiselessly over the wastes which I was now treading; while, had concealment

from view been desirable on the part of anyone, the heath-clad surface, the large clumps
of furze scattered here and there, and the
mist which still continued to hang in clouds
and patches around, afforded endless facility.

The reader is at liberty to form what ideas
he may please on the amount of fortitude
evinced by me on this occasion. Truth
obliges me to confess that the feeling, having
its source in fact or fancy, of being thus
watched, and my footsteps followed, through
these dreary wastes and partial obscurity,
came, in time, to take so firm a hold upon
me as to threaten, if much longer indulged
in, to prove well-nigh intolerable. Reason,
it is true, assured me that no attempt on my
life could be intended ; if it were really a gun
which I was under the belief of beholding,
its unseen owner had had abundant opportunities for lodging its contents in my body ;
for I had not the least doubt that I was now
in the midst of a large and uninhabited tract,
and the mist, even thus rent and partially
dispersed, still lingered in sufficient force to
render all objects invisible at any considerable

distance. My assassination would therefore be unseen; while the report of firearms—if heard at all, a most unlikely supposition—would, doubtless, be attributed to the gun of a fowler, or some citizen sportsman come out from the neighbouring metropolis for a day's shooting. Simple robbery without violence—or with the least violence possible —was not perhaps a supposition so untenable as the former. But setting aside the security of the empty, or comparatively empty, traveller, I had the further one of considering myself quite competent to cope, hand to hand, with a single assailant: and no stretch of my fancy had hitherto conjured up more than one cap, and one barrel of a gun, at a time. But if apprehension was thus slight, or groundless, on the score of reason, the powers of the imagination are not at all times amenable to its control. And thus, while all idea of spiritual or ghostly agency was the farthest from my thoughts, one good look, face to face, at a real man, with a cap and a gun, would have done more to reassure me than all my efforts of pure argument.

Having continued my journey for some time under these far from agreeable sensations, I at length, and as a last resource, formed the resolve to put an end to them by fixedly, and more permanently, concentrating my ideas on some other subject. My best course of proceeding in the face of the coming night, being that one which most appropriately presented itself to me, I determined to give my whole mind to its consideration. With which purpose, I took my seat on a neighbouring knoll, the highest I could find.

I looked to the sun, and found—as well as I could define the position of that luminary—that he had yet some hours to run; besides which, I might fairly calculate on an hour or so of twilight. I was obliged to confess to myself that symptoms of fatigue were already making themselves known to me; but, on a pinch, I felt equal to a few hours' more walking—my only perplexity being whither to direct my steps; or, in other words, by what course lay the most feasible exit from this cheerless tract. I could have no doubt now that I had wandered into that elevated

plateau, which (so Captain Ogleby had informed me) traversed the whole of the central
portion of Wicklow, entering at its northern
boundary, and making its exit through the
southern confines of the county.   On the
other hand, the east and west portions of the
county, running on either side of this central
strip, were (the same informant had given
me to understand) considerably lower, and
contained good level soil.   As I approached
either of these side portions, I had little
doubt that I would soon fall in with human
habitations again.   Thus my most advisable
course evidently lay in pursuing a direct
path, due east or west, as long as my powers
of endurance enabled me.   The sun was now
sinking toward the west, and so far might be
taken as a pretty tolerable guide in adhering
to a straight line.   The task before me was
by no means inviting.   But it was the best
—if not the only one—which suggested itself
to me ; and I started up, with fresh alacrity,
to enter upon it.

For the first half-hour or so, the country
continued to preserve the same appearance

of flat unprofitable bog, bearing the like plentiful crop of heath. But, gradually, I became aware that I was entering upon a more hilly portion. I passed some eminences on my right hand and left; and others, of much greater altitude, lay before me. Gazing on their heights, I was paying but slight attention to the intervening space, when suddenly I found myself on the margin of a small circular lake, and perceived my course in that direction completely arrested. Indeed, the body of water on which I now looked was enclosed on all quarters—except that by which I had gained access to it—by lofty mountainous sides; and, had I been able by any means to cross the lake, all further progress up these perfectly precipitous heights seemed impossible. The contents of the lake were of the deepest tinge which I had yet seen, doubtless from the peaty character of the soil; and the inclosing sides, or walls, rising out of the water, and towering high above, added in no small degree to invest the whole scene with a singularly gloomy appearance. Nay,

the sun—as it were to intensify this latter
effect—was just then sinking behind the
overhanging mountain which rose on the
side of the lake opposite to me, and flung a
gigantic shadow across the surface of the
water, and far into the heath-covered shore
on which I was standing. I gazed on him
as long as a portion of his disk was visible,
not without a certain feeling of fascination :
with his swift disappearance—and I could
almost mark the progress of his descent
behind the mountain—my last hope of
escape from these inhospitable wilds seemed
passing away. Another moment, and he
had plunged out of view. The vast black
mass of the mountain lay between me and
the luminary, and I turned for relief toward
the other objects of the landscape. For the
first time, I now perceived a human figure
standing within a few feet of me. My
previous preoccupation, and the springy
nature of the soil already alluded to, were
quite enough in themselves to account for
the approach of this person being unnoticed
by me—had any thoughts of a ghostly, or

immaterial, nature obtained previous hold
on my mind, or now found admission from
the singularly sombre and desolate character
of the scene which surrounded us. But the
appearance of the individual which now met
my gaze—though sufficiently striking and
remarkable at any period or place—was
calculated at once to convince me that I had
a real person of flesh and blood to deal with;
while the attitude, manner, and bearing were
certainly more those of one who stood
on the defensive—and habitually so stood—
than those of an actual aggressor. I make
this explanation more in reference to previous sensations, already recorded by me,
than to any apprehension which so sudden
an apparition in the midst of these dreary
wastes might be calculated to draw forth ;
once thus brought face to face with mortal
mould, my principal idea was that of aid
in escaping from my hitherto purposeless
wanderings.

The person who now stood within a yard
or so of me, on the margin of this dark and
motionless body cf water, might be about

six feet, or nearly six feet in stature—though
an apparently habitual stoop in his shoulders
deprived him of an inch or so of his natural
height.   Notwithstanding this stoop, however, and some stoutness of form, his appearance gave indications of considerable bodily
activity.   His complexion was ruddy, and a
lively, clear, and penetrating eye—which
was now by no means unobservant of my
movements—contributed to create an impression not at all unfavourable in the mind
of the beholder.   In social position, I should
have placed him somewhat above that of the
peasantry whom I had yet met—and, indeed,
a certain air of decision, and even of authority, aided to elevate him still further above
this class.   A gun, the stock of which rested
on the turf at his foot, the barrel being held
lightly in his left hand, might have given
him the appearance of a fowler; to which
impression, a bag, or netting, slung round
his shoulder, and stocked to repletion with
hares, widgeon, snipe, and other game (in
which I had previously ample testimony that
these mountainous tracts abounded), lent

additional colouring. But a brace of pistols equally conspicuous in the belt which encompassed his waist was not similarly explainable, while a semi-transparent horn, rudely fashioned into a shot-pouch at one end, was sufficiently capacious to afford suspicions of other more bulky contents, in the shape of ball cartridge, at the other and larger extremity. As his left hand maintained the barrel of the gun in its upright position, I was able to observe that it was to some slight extent injured, though evidently not to such a degree as to hinder its owner making use of it. In England, the word " poacher " might have possibly risen to my lips on contemplating this figure. But I had previously heard from my friend, Captain Ogleby, that no efforts had been as yet made to preserve these tracts of mountain and bog—at all events, on their Wicklow side ; and that they were free to all who could command the necessary time and materials for bagging their game. Here, then, a poacher, in the ordinary acceptation of the term, could have no real existence.

My chief impression in gazing on this somewhat singular-looking person was that plain dealing held out to me the best, and indeed only hope of quieting suspicion and obtaining my needful information. Without any appearance of show, his eyes had been hitherto narrowly scanning my movements, and, so far from making advance, he had, as yet, not even recognised my presence by word or gesture—a most unusual proceeding, I had already opportunities for observing, among the Irish peasantry and small-farmer class, whose ready "God save you kindly," seldom failed to meet the wayfarer's ear.

"I started from Dublin, this morning, and have lost my way among these mountains."

"Naithless," was the sole exclamation of my new acquaintance, apparently uttered under the impression that my statement was quite superfluous, and that I had yet to come to the gist of the matter.

"I am bound for Ravensdale House—can you put me on the straight course again? I am a relative of Mr. Allen Featherstone."

" Ay—that's true enough. Your Saxon
tongue can't hide a Featherstone."

Somewhat encouraged by this recognition
(if I might so understand it) of the truth of
my assertion—whether attributable to face,
figure, or manner I was ignorant—I was
about to repeat my request, when the stranger
again proceeded,—

" You are now ten good miles from the
Glen of the Ravens—and have been turning your back upon it for some hours.
Are you man enough for the journey, when
you are put on the road?"—And he of the
gun glanced at my travel-stained limbs in a
manner which seemed to infer little doubt
as to the answer which conscience must
prompt.

In truth, after a whole day spent in walking and strict fast, ten such miles as these
I had more lately waded through, and under
impending night, did appear to me to lie
beyond my present powers of endurance.
Without any direct reply, therefore, I turned
to some less doubtful alternative.

" Is there not some house of entertainment

nearer, then? — I have not met any
signs of human habitation for some hours
now."

"Nor will—for some hours to come. You
are now in the midst of an uninhabited bog,
stretching away for miles on every side of
you."

Where the person who thus addressed me
intended to make his own residence for the
coming night—or whether he felt his legs
sufficiently strong to carry him to more hospitable regions—was a consideration which
naturally occurred to my mind, but which I
forbore to give voice to, as savouring too
strongly of the inquisitive. Again, therefore, I was obliged to turn to other possibi-
lities of the case.

"Then, there remains nothing for it but
to pass the night on the heath?"

"It is not come to that with a Featherstone yet. There is another course—but on
conditions."

"And what may those conditions be?"

"That you use not your eyes now—nor
your tongue hereafter! Are these terms

less inviting than a supperless bed, and the
mountain mist for your blanket?"

I confess the allusion to supper (my breakfast had been a very early one), however
vague and indirect it might be accounted,
went a very considerable way toward mode-
rating the startling nature of this proposal.
Yet, as his conditions were couched in somewhat enigmatical language (I had already
observed that, whether from habit or inclination, the stranger seemed to encourage a
certain abruptness, and even sententiousness,
of style in his ordinary address), I was not
disinclined to learn his meaning more fully.

"As to my silence, I can have no objection to make promise of that—so long as I
am not made a participator in any illegal act.
How to prevent my eyes from seeing, I confess I cannot so clearly understand—unless
I blindfold them?"

The stranger made a slight inclination of
his head—the first I had yet observed—as
if in acknowledgment of my readiness of
apprehension—and then added—"I have
trusted my life, young man, on the word of

a Featherstone ere now, and am willing to do so again. But I am not at equal liberty to expose the lives and secrets of others, however small I may account the risk. Follow me blindfolded, or follow not at all."

These words were said not without an air of rough, native dignity; whatever hesitation I might have previously had to trust myself so implicitly into the hands of a stranger, they went far, at least, by the air of sincerity and truth which they carried with them, to remove any impression of personal danger to myself. It was, therefore, in all probability with a view to tone down any appearance of a too ready acceptance, that I found myself making reply — it may be, too, in somewhat of his own style—so infectious is mannerism.

" You may account your affairs as still in your own keeping, so far as tongue of mine is concerned. The falling night appears to me about to place a like restraint upon my eyesight, without resort to other means."

"There are two good hours to night yet,"

said the stranger. "The Keeper stands between us and daylight; on the other side of
the mountain, the sun is yet high in the
heavens. But use your eyes" (doubtless,
from long habit, as well, perhaps, as natural
penetration, he had already perceived that it
was my intention to accept his terms,) "as
long as you may—the way here is rough, and
you will have to traverse it alone in the
morning. When we approach our destination, I will speak — after that, I hold a
Featherstone's word."

So saying, he turned from the spot, and led
the way, for some time, in a southern direction, so I was able to learn from the position
of the sun; which, as soon as we had advanced out of the shadow of the huge mountain mass, did indeed appear still high in
the sky.

Half an hour's brisk walking brought us
to the entrance of a valley, between two
neighbouring hills, up which my companion
proceeded; and, on our arrival at its termi-
ation, or rather gradual opening out into a
heath-covered plain, informed me that I must

now enter upon the conditions proposed by
him.　I bound a handkerchief tightly around
my temples, and we again proceeded at a
somewhat slower pace.

An indistinct noise, which had been gradually gaining in strength as we continued our
progress, was now sufficiently audible to inform me that it proceeded from a body of
falling water; and, in a short time, it became
evident that we were bearing down upon it.
Indeed, at a sudden turn of the path, the
sound struck upon my ear with redoubled
force, and I conjectured that we could not be
many paces from one of those cascades, which
tumbling from a great height, and almost
perpendicularly, furnish so frequent a feature
of this portion of the country ; deriving their
thunders more from the high precipitous
nature of their fall, than the comparatively
small volume of water they possess—at least,
in the summer season.　At this point, my
companion took me by the arm ; but, so far
from diverging from the direction of the
waterfall, we appeared to me to be actually
advancing into it.

"If," said the stranger, "he were not a
Featherstone I held, I would say, fear not.
Your forefathers feared neither man nor
devil."

Whether assured by his words, or desirous
of upholding the honour of the family name—
now unexpectedly intrusted to my keeping—
I spoke not, and endeavoured to direct my
advance with as little appearance of hesitation as possible. I could have little doubt
now that we were actually passing, or about
to pass, behind the body of falling water—
that is, *between* the cascade and the high rock
or ledge to which it owed its origin. The
thunder resounded in my ears, a light
spray plentifully bedewed my cheek, a sharp
turn seemed to cut off the wild din of waters
behind us; and my companion informed me
that I was again at liberty to use my eyes.

CHAPTER VIII.

UNEXPECTED QUARTERS.

THE permission did not seem likely to be of much avail to me at first. I could barely perceive that I stood in the middle of a large cavern or grotto, formed, apparently by nature, in the solid rock; but the very small amount of light at my disposal was insufficient to enable me to distinguish clearly any of the objects which it contained. A light, however, there was, and I had little difficulty in tracing its source (assisted, as I was, by my olfactory nerves, which assured me of the presence of peat smoke) to a few sods of turf which smouldered in a portion of the cave—doubtless used as a fireplace. I could further perceive the dim outline of my companion, bending over this fireplace,

or, rather, hearth—for the embers rested on
the solid rock flooring of the cavern—and
endeavouring, by help of one of the burning
sods, to ignite a strip of wood—which my
Irish lore led me at once to conjecture to be
the native " bog-deal," so generally used by
the peasantry of the more retired districts as
a substitute for candles. And truly, had I
much of an eye for picturesque effect at the
time, the scene at this portion of the chamber was not unworthy of a glance. In one
hand, the stranger held the partially burning
sod, in the other the strip of bog-deal ; and
blew the former (no ordinary bellows, I am
sure, ever emitted so long, so continuous,
and so steady a blast), until he had raised a
red glow, and eventually a flame ; while his
bending form, with its half-sportsman, half-
lawless appearance—the glare thrown full on
his face in its close proximity to the burning
peat, and reflecting a set of features (his head
was now uncovered), neither unprepossessing
nor unintellectual—and the various other
portions of the cavern exhibiting each its
distinct   hue   of   impenetrable   darkness,

gloom, and partial light,—all went to the
formation of a picture which might have
well merited the attention of a painter seeking suggestions in the mysteries of light and
shade. Presently, he had succeeded in his
efforts, and attaching the flaming strip to a
very primitive-looking candlestick (to wit, a
moveable upright post, or pillar, of wood,
standing about a yard high, and placed in
the middle of the floor), he next proceeded
to divest himself of his game-bag, pouch, etc.

The whole chamber was now fully lit up,
and as my host appeared to place no restraint
whatever on my observation (indeed, having
once obtained my promise, or implication of
a promise, he seemed to give himself no
further concern about the matter), I threw a
glance around it.

Means of egress I saw none, and was at
some loss to understand how we had effected
an entrance. A pot, or vessel, hung suspended over the smouldering sods, attached
by a short and very smoke-begrimed chain,
to a staple driven into the solid rock. And
as my companion, moving about the apart-

ment, approached from time to time the
fireplace, and raised the lid, an odour, not
altogether uninviting, diffused itself through
the chamber, and contended for a moment
with the pungency of the peat smoke :
chimney or flue I saw none, and this latter,
after disporting itself around the upper walls
and roof, converting the natural colour of
the rock into a deep black, went—I knew
not how, or whither. In one corner lay a
pile, or "stack," of peat-sods, from which,
among his other offices, my companion had
already replenished the fire ; while, in another corner, was an equally large pile of
dry heath. A few volumes of books, on a
stone ledge, also attracted my attention (the
more so, as the rudimentary art of reading
was by no means so widespread among the
lower ranks at the period of my tale as at
present), throwing, as they did, some light
on the general propriety of language which
was not altogether to be expected from the
appearance of the stranger. A rude table,
and an equally rude pair of stools pretty
nearly completed the contents of the

chamber. It held no other occupant; though, from one or two smaller articles scattered about—of a less home-made, and, indeed, superior manufacture—it was open to conjecture whether such was always the case.

Having completed these preliminary arrangements, the duties of hospitality appeared now to recur to the mind of my conductor. He addressed me in a manner less constrained; though his words and bearing never entirely lost that air—whether of distance or reserve — which had first arrested my attention. This air I am unable better to describe than as a compound of independence and that deference which persons in the more humble classes of life usually render (and more markedly in Ireland) to those whom they consider above them in social station; tinged, certainly, with a dash of cynicism, which might be natural, or the acquirement by such habits of isolation as all around me bore testimony of.

"There are roasted potatoes in the ashes,"

said he, "if your mountain wanderings will
permit no longer delay"—and suiting the
action to the word, he disclosed, by disturbing the half-red peat embers, a number of
those tubers—"but, if you can parry with
your appetite for some half-hour longer, you
may have a dish more fitting to stay a gentle
stomach."

My pangs of hunger certainly caused
themselves to be sufficiently felt. But
whether desirous to still uphold in my
person the endurance of a Featherstone, or
that the pot continued to exhale so savoury
a vapour, as my companion added from time
to time to its contents the hare, a wild duck,
and some smaller wild-fowl, I expressed my
ability to await the half-hour and its results,
at the same time, taking a seat on one of the
stools.

The stranger, having now completed his
arrangements, and piled a large pyramid of
turf around the boiling cauldron, retired for
a moment to a recess of the cavern, and
straightway reappeared again with a small
wooden vessel—a "noggin," I understood

him to call it—the contents of which, when brought more immediately under my nose, I had no hesitation in pronouncing as similar to that which I had already discussed, for the first time, on the preceding evening, by the invitation, and with the assistance, of Captain Ogleby.

"It will take the cold mist out of your stomach," said my companion, "and put heat into your limbs again."

I would have pleaded for the addition of a little water; but ignorant how far in this matter I might be transgressing the traditional usages of my family, I made essay to gulp down a portion of the contents, though as a consequence my eyes swam, and for some moments the contest between wind and windpipe was acute, if not even alarming.

"It's good—it's not to be denied," said my companion, who seemed to view these symptoms as unqualified approval of the excellence of the liquid—"Paudeen Gow never deceived me yet;" and he drained the contents of the vessel, though without

any similar results manifesting themselves—
"I'll be bound you feel the heat rising in
you?"

I certainly did—more especially about the
throat and air passages—but these favourable effects were more than counterbalanced
by the pangs of hunger which now attacked
me with redoubled force; nor was it without something very like a sigh of relief that
I saw the stranger place a portion of the
contents of the cauldron on the table before
me, flanked by a goodly array of the roasted
tubers. Having made these arrangements
on my behalf, he provided himself with a
similar portion, and retiring with the remaining stool to a distant portion of the
chamber, prepared to do justice to the
results of his own gastronomic skill.

This separation of our small forces took, I
confess, somewhat from the ardour of my
first attack. The stranger could, it is true,
in no ordinary acceptation of the term, be
taken as belonging to the same social rank
in life as myself—and the fact had been
sufficiently and spontaneously indicated by

himself, even in his more independent and reserved moments. Nevertheless, I had expected that the peculiar circumstances under which we met would have somewhat levelled this distinction for the time being. I went the length of remarking that the board was large enough for us two—but his only reply was,—

"Eat on—it is your right; better than I have sat below the salt of the Featherstones, ere now. In this country, it is not the custom for gentleman and peasant to play table companions together."

"In my country," said I, unwilling to detect any aspersion on my native land which his words might, or might not, be intended to convey—"the peasantry are but little given to such pursuits"—and I pointed to the row of books already alluded to by me.

"Nevertheless, I am a peasant, the son of a peasant—though my father, poor man, endeavoured to give me some advantages— and a book has, at times, proved a needful companion here. Caves and dens are for the wild beasts of the earth ; perhaps, but for such help, I might have become more of the wild beast than I am.''

After this speech—a somewhat long, less abrupt, and unusually confidential one for him—he again resumed his meal; and, whether this allusion to family matters, or that to his isolated life, had called up unpleasant reminiscences, he made no attempt to renew the conversation for some time.

Whatever scruples, however, my companion might entertain on the score of eating in my immediate company, he seemed to have more slight ones on the head of drinking. On the conclusion of the meal, he drew his stool close to the fire, filled a very short and very black pipe with tobacco, and having ignited it by crushing the bowl down on a red ember which he drew forward on the hearth from the burning pile for that purpose, he replenished his "noggin," and, from time to time, had recourse to its contents with apparent relish, and some air of relaxation, between the pauses of his smoking. Nor, in the meantime, was he unmindful of his guest.

"Up at the Big House" (intimating, as I conjectured by the motion of his hand, my uncle's residence) "you'll be sitting down to French claret after your meal—the quality must have their fancies; for myself, both taste and colour too closely remind me of bog-water, and there's small scarcity of that hereabouts. Now, if you would try this, warmed up with a taste of boiling water (maybe, Paudeen Gow did make it a trifle over-proof this time—the gauger does not often pay him a visit, and he has no more liking for bog-water than myself) you'll sleep the sounder for it, and may defy cramps and agues."

But my recollection of the effects of Mr. Gow's fire-water were as yet too fresh, and I resolutely refused further trial under any form. During the remaining time I sat by the hearth, we spoke little, the stranger being, to all appearances, busied with his own thoughts. Without, the night threatened to be a rough one; already the wind came moaning up the surrounding glens, mingling its cadences with the dull and diminished plashings of the waterfall. Occasionally, a more shrill and piercing blast found its way to the very entrance—as my conjectures led me to place it—of our strange abode, drowning for the moment all other sound, and then retired to wail piteously in the distance.

" Hear to it!—hear to it !" more than once broke from my companion at such periods, apparently in reference to the wind itself—"that's great grief."

The words were evidently spoken without intention to produce rejoinder, and, indeed, seemed the mere utterance of his own thoughts and meditations. Once, I was so far tempted as to reply that "the sounds did indeed, at times, seem almost those of a human being." But he shook his head— said " No, no,—there's no human voice there," and relapsed into his former silence.

Presently, I intimated my wish to retire for the night, urging as plea my weary day's wanderings, and the necessity for an early start in the morning. My host placed a strip of lighted bog-deal in my hand ; and,

having conducted me to an inner recess of
the cave, which had hitherto escaped my
notice, and pointed to a quantity of heath
which lay there, and which he now proceeded
to shake out in the form of a couch, informed
me that it was to be my bed for the night.

"It's fresh gathered and dry—you can at
least say that for one night you have had
the heather for your bed."

I turned for a moment to survey my apartment, if it might be so called—door there
was none, and, indeed, the recess was but a
further natural enlargement in the cavern,
but an enlargement in such a direction as to
interrupt the view between itself and the
outer portion. It contained no furniture
whatever, and a glance sufficed to inform me
that my couch, and a pair of pistols, which
were suspended by a leathern thong from
the wall, or side, of the cavern, were the sole
contents of the chamber. Under a somewhat
liberal rendering of the terms imposed upon
me by the strange occupant of this abode, I
approached these latter for the purpose of a
nearer inspection. They were small and of

most elegant workmanship, evidently French, and wholly differing, in style and quality, from anything else I had seen in the cave, with the exception of one or two articles already alluded to. They were loaded, and the priming appeared quite fresh. The silver mounting extended round the whole stock, and on the butt end of each were inscribed the letters " R. E." The initials were wholly unfamiliar to me, and conjecture failed to suggest for what name they stood. Little could I dream how familiar that name was yet to become, or how intimately associated with my future narrative its owner was to be.

But my pine-strip burned low. There was actually nothing else in the small chamber for me to examine; and, throwing myself on my heath-couch, I was soon, thanks to a long and weary day's wanderings, buried in deep sleep.

CHAPTER IX.

I AWOKE with a bright light playing full on my face; nor could I have the least doubt that it was that of the sun, though I was, as yet, unconscious how it could gain access to my small chamber. In truth, it needed some moments' reflection to bring before my mind where I really was. Little more than eight-and-forty hours ago in England, yesterday in Dublin, and now sleeping securely in a real cavern, in the midst of a real Irish bog, and the guest of a man who could certainly be on no very favourable terms of intimacy with the legal authorities of the island! How would my thoroughly respectable father—how would my English-minded mother regard such proceedings?

Or was it any wonder that I should question myself whether this moving panorama of events was not a mere dream? A dream! (so ran the current of my thoughts)—surely I *had* a dream last night; or was *it*, too, one of those actual and real events which I was now trying to arrange in order, in my somewhat confused brain, with a view to become more clear as to my present position? Yes; a dream, or an actual occurrence, I could certainly call to mind, between my lying down last night and my waking with this burst of sun-light playing on my face. Methought I lay in a half-sleeping, half-waking state, as it were on my present heather-couch. The light was much less strong; but there was some light. Presently, a young man—so, at least, the slight and agile figure would lead me to infer—entered my chamber, with a quick and active step; and, passing lightly by my bed (it might be to escape observation, or from an unwillingness to break in on my slumbers) approached the opposite wall. After a few moments, he re-passed by the same way, and the chamber was again empty; nor could I call to mind anything further until I now found myself awake, and sitting up on my heather-bed.

On further reflecting over the night's experience, I was the more inclined to set this incident down as no mere coinage of the brain, but an actual and real occurrence; though other proof than that I have already mentioned for such a supposition, I found none. The lights—both the light which I saw now, and the fainter light which I had seen, or supposed myself to have seen, during the night—I was still unable to account for, though my further researches after rising— presently to be recounted—appeared to offer some explanation of these latter pheno- mena.

On leaving my novel resting-place, and proceeding into the outward chamber, I found my companion of the preceding day employed in the preparation of the morning meal. He informed me that the hour was somewhat late; but that, as I had appeared to sleep soundly, he had, in consideration of my fatigue of yesterday, refrained from waking

me—" A couple of hours' fair walking ought
to bring you and Glen-na-Fiac more nearly
acquainted ; and you must have no fears for
the mountain-mist to-day. If you would feel
the fresher for a bath, you may have one
at hand,"—and, at the same time, he
pointed to the back portion of the cave,
where the light appeared to gain ingress.
Proceeding in the direction (I had little
doubt in concluding that it was *not* the
way by which we had entered), I found the
cave to gradually retire, until, losing its roof,
it resolved itself into a deep gorge, or cleft,
between two perfectly precipitous, and nearly
meeting, sides. A small stream trickled at
the bottom of this fissure, making its exit by
a still more subterraneous passage by the side
of the cavern, instead of entering it. As I
looked up the long and narrow vista—a thin
thread of blue sky merely disclosing itself
overhead—I felt more certain still that there
could be no exit by that way. A border, or
fringe, of pine-trees, moreover, clung along
the topmost ridge of each side, adding still
further to the apparent height of the cleft;

and the peat-smoke from the cavern, partly lost along the walls of the gorge, was further wholly dispersed among the foliage of the latter, none appearing to reach the upper air. I had passed some similar gorges during my wanderings of the previous day; and, whether caused by a sudden disruption, or (the more usual explanation) by the slow action, through ages, of the small streams which trickle through them, they are, I believe, a generally diffused feature of the district.

I was now able to obtain some clue as to the lighting of the cave. The sun, in the morning, shining down this cleft, would send a portion of his beams into the cavern; and, during *all* periods of the day, a smaller quantity of his light, reflected from the sides of the gorge, would find similar entrance. The sun rose, at this season of the year, a little after three o'clock; and there would be some twilight even before that hour. I could not, therefore, have been many hours in bed before some portion of the dawning light had gained access to my chamber; and it was, in all probability, this light which had disturbed my slumbers (I was now quite convinced that it was no dream I had experienced), and temporarily roused me to a half-conscious, half-waking state; after which, I must have slept to a later period of the morning.

I refreshed myself in the cool running stream, as it brawled and fretted down its rocky channel; and, having made what toilet circumstances permitted, rejoined my companion. We ate our meal in comparative silence; nor was allusion made to the occurrences of the night—and but slight to those of the preceding day.

In a short time, the stranger informed me that he was ready to accompany me on a portion of the way; and, taking his gun and game-bag, he preceded me toward a part of the cavern where I could perceive no visible outlet. Not so, however, my companion; for, displacing an ingeniously-fitted compartment or panel, formed of the native turf ("scraw," I have since heard it called by the peasantry, who use it for roofing their cabins), he disclosed an aperture sufficiently wide to permit our egress. Of my own accord, I

again bound the handkerchief across my
eyes; nor did I remove it until my companion
informed me I was at liberty to do so.

I have already lost so much time about
those dreary wastes that—fortunately for the
reader's patience—I need say little further
of my journey through them to-day. The
solitary incident worth recording occurred as
—after wending our way through a long and
very lonely glen, and in complete silence—
we came out on its termination in an equally
deserted patch of moorland. Here, and as
it were to guard the entrance of the glen, a
pile of buildings had at some period—to all
appearances not a remote one—been constructed. Nothing now remained standing,
however, save a solitary gable here and
there; while portions of the main walls,
broken into blocks of masonry, and scattered
—many to a considerable distance—suggested that some great and sudden force had
been applied, instead of the more slow hand
of Time. Hitherto, our journey had been
conducted under so little conversation that I
might, in all probability, have passed this scene

of desolation—highly suggestive, indeed, in itself of silence—did it not appear to me that a smile of some peculiar meaning flitted across the features of my companion, as his eye rested for a moment on these blackened ruins.

" A lonely spot for a house," I exclaimed.

" Ay—too lonely: so the man thought that knocked it down."

" Indeed!" said I ; " apparently, it is a modern structure. Was the owner, then, dissatisfied with his plan ? "

" No—his neighbours were; one of them, at least."

·" Ah!" said I, in lieu of better exclamation. " And yet this one dissatisfied individual must have had others to assist him ? These blocks of masonry were formed for strength —here are the remains of loopholes for musketry."

" Not a man—not a finger but his own," said the stranger, with some energy.

" Or equally powerful appliances, then ? "

" Ay—that is nearer to the mark. Put a couple of kegs of gunpowder under that tall rock that rises before you, and you may see something of the same effect." After which words, the stranger again relapsed into silence; nor did I make any further effort to interrupt the train of his thoughts.

After a couple of hours' smart walking, the whole surface of the country began to assume an entire change of appearance. Our progress was now down-hill, and the slopes and flanks of the high plateau we were quitting afforded some highly picturesque views. Occasionally, I found myself turning to catch a look of some new combination of mountain, streamlet, and glen. Nor was the country we were descending into less refreshing, of its kind, to the eye. Below us lay an extensive lowland, fertile, cultivated, and thickly interspersed with habitations. Here, a country seat appeared in the midst of a thickly-wooded vale; there, a peaceful hamlet sent up its smoke on high; while, beyond all, lay the Irish Channel, bearing a goodly array of sail on its surface.

"Yes," said my companion, in answer to some exclamation of mine, "you now behold the garden of Wicklow. You know what the Dean" (the Dean, I found—and he is no infrequent authority among the peasantry—invariably meant Dean Swift) "says of our county—'a frieze mantle, fringed with gold.' The frieze is for such as I—and here I must leave you to complete your journey alone. Carry your eye along yonder strip of pine plantation, and you will see, a little beyond it, a large square house, with lawn in front intersected by a sheet of water. That is the Big House of Glen-na-fiac, the Valley of the Ravens—or Ravensdale, as later fashion has it."

My guide, I had already observed, always used the native appellation in referring to my uncle's residence, or, at least, some strictly literal interpretation of it, and seldom heard the more modern title without betraying signs of disapproval.

I had no difficulty in following his directions with my eye, and saw that, by availing myself of the pine plantation referred to, I would stand almost over the house. A more considerable difficulty in my mind was, in

what manner to part with my companion.
Pecuniary recompense, I plainly saw, was
out of the question. Nothing, it is true,
that I had yet seen could lead me to infer
that he was over-burdened with this world's
riches. Nevertheless, his independent manner, his reserve on his own affairs, and a
general air of distance which, at no time, had
he entirely laid aside—all induced me to
believe that such a return for his services
would be displeasing to him, and would
stand in danger of rejection. It appeared,
therefore, to be my most advisable course to
simply thank him for the assistance he had
rendered me, accompanying my thanks with
a hope (Heaven forgive the slight dissimula-
tion!—I had my doubts whether he *could*
descend into those more peaceful-looking
lowlands) that I would shortly see him at my
uncle's residence. I turned from my contemplation of Ravensdale House, for the
purpose of carrying out this intention, but
the stranger was already scaling a neighbouring acclivity, down which we had just
descended. He must have seen my move-

ment—his quick glance, I had more than once observed, marked much less conspicuous objects in the course of our journey. But he made no corresponding gesture; and, in another moment, the overhanging foliage had completely hidden him.'

Left thus to myself, I had time to take a more leisurely survey of the object of my late wanderings, as also to satisfy some natural curiosity. I could have no doubt that I gazed on one of those extensive structures, raised by the Irish country gentleman of the preceding century, when, it is to be inferred, the times were more in accord with his largeness of heart. Howbeit, evidence was not wanting that these better times had already passed away, as regarded the Valley of the Ravens.

The house stood in the midst of a district partly woodland, and partly agricultural. The coach-road ran in front of the structure, on the opposite side of the lawn already mentioned—if a somewhat extensive enclosure, now consisting of waving meadow, might merit that appellation. The piece of

ornamental water, to which my late companion had directed my attention, was an
artificial extension of one of the many small
streams which trickled down the flanks of the
mountain range, from which I had descended.
It ran for some time along the side of the
road farthest from the house—I could even
trace it back, through some smaller meadow-
flats, until, beside a rustic summer-house,
now fallen into much decay, it issued, in its
natural form, from the pine plantation.
Following the forward course of this artificial
cutting, I found that, after wending its way
through these meadow-flats, it crossed the
road by means of a single low arch; and,
continuing its course through the larger
meadow, or lawn, finally terminated, after
sending off a couple of branches, within a
few yards of the house.   It was constructed
sufficiently wide for boating purposes, but
the whole of its surface was now covered
with duck-weed and wild aquatic plants.
Duck-weed, bulrushes, flaggers, and reeds
do not perhaps enhance the appearance
of ornamental water-courses in country

gentlemen's pleasure-grounds ; but, in the
present instance, they certainly took away
from the one before me all air of *newness*,
and thus made it to accord more nearly with
the house and its surroundings. The lawn
itself was diversified by hill and dale—considerably assisted by art, too, if I might
judge from the configuration of the district
immediately adjoining; and a glorious
avenue of beech, with two or three clumps
of enormous copper-coloured beech scattered
here and there, considerably added to its
picturesque effect. More minute details,
however, and a nearer inspection (I found
that I could keep the house under my eye in
proceeding along the pine plantation, and
was now doing so) told wofully against this
somewhat imposing outline. The lawn had
evidently been laid out, at some by-gone
period, with a view to floricultural as well
as arboricultural effect; and, amid the wild
foxglove and lady's-slipper of the meadow,
were still to be seen—here, a tender nar-
cissus, there a solitary moss-rose, and, anon,
the gorgeous cup of a tulip (looking more

red for very indignation)—contending with
their more hardy brethren of the field and
woodland. Some attempt, it is true, was
still maintained in the immediate neighbourhood of the house to preserve the appearance
of a former state of things; but it would
seem as if the task were somewhat beyond
the strength of the hand which had under-
taken it—was it a woman's?—and a flower-
bed or two hardly maintained its ground
against the encroaching mead. An avenue,
destitute of trees,—the beech avenue lay
on the opposite side of the house, and was
evidently intended merely as a walk for
pedestrians—conducted to the entrance, de-
positing the traveller on a gravel-sweep in
front of some stone steps. The house itself
was a plain square building, remarkable only
for its size. Traces of age were by no means
wanting; and, sooth to say, they appeared,
of late years, to have met no corresponding
effort to hide them. Yet the whole structure, it was evident to be seen, had been
originally built strongly and substantially,
and might be pronounced serviceable yet,

for many a year to come, with a little outlay and care. A semicircle of offices, enclosing an enormous court-yard, lay at the rear of the building; and some ricks of hay and stacks of corn there attested that farming operations were still carried on; while the usual huge rick of turf was also conspicuous.

But the great orchard was, perhaps, the sight which most attracted my eye. *There*, age had only added a thicker coating of moss to the forest of fruit-trees, enhancing their appearance in my eyes; while neglect had but made the hazel-paths more shady, the immense walnut-trees more towering, and the thickets—I could call them nought else—of currant, gooseberry, and raspberry-bushes, still more impenetrable. The apple and pear-trees now presented vast mounds of pink and white blossoms, and the tangled strawberry-beds gave similar promise of fruit in their season.

My peripatetic examination had brought me to the extremity of the upland pine plantation, which ceased at the commence-

ment of the meadow-flats just mentioned.
Crossing over the little brawling streamlet,
which issued from its cool retreat, I entered
the summer-house. The pines had here, in
a measure, given place to a hazel-copse, and,
amid its redundancy of foliage and silver-
barked boughs, the small building stood. It
had evidently been constructed after the
pagoda fashion; though—all pieces of mere
ornamentation, with, here and there, a more
necessary board or two, having been long
since removed (doubtless by the neighbouring
peasantry, in "a bad turf season," for the
purposes of fuel)—there might be some difficulty in determining this, on a first inspection. A still more neglected boat-house
stood adjacent; in which (I was about to
write, under the protection of which) a small
boat lay, moored by a rusty chain. A row
of seating ran round the inside of the summer house; and, being formed of thicker
slabs, more securely fastened, had better
withstood time and spoliation, though the
door had long since disappeared, and some
boughs of an adjacent hazel-tree had in-

truded themselves through the window. The seats—indeed, almost *all* portions of the woodwork were indented with a great number of initials (some rudely cut, some more artistically carved; some bearing traces—I might almost say of antiquity, and others of comparatively recent formation), in which the letter " F"—intended, I could not doubt, for our family name—entered into combination with almost every other letter of the alphabet. A venerable " P. F." I had no difficulty in attributing to the Sir Percy Featherstone already mentioned by my late companion, Captain Ogleby, as an old holder of the title. A "D. F." was, doubtless, the work of Sir Digges, the present baronet — though evidently executed many years ago ; and, if I might judge from the attempt, at a somewhat juvenile period of his life. Another, and a quite differently executed " D. F." I at once set down as my father's—a conclusion which the date (the self-same year in which he had obtained his commission, and departed from Ireland), appended to one of these latter inscriptions, further confirmed ;

and an " A. F." I apportioned to my uncle,
the Allen Featherstone whom I was now
about to behold for the first time : nay, in
the course of my researches, I came across
these three lost names, or initials of names,
forming a sort of Round Robin ; within
which I could trace " July, 1768," executed,
doubtless, during some school vacation.
Nor could I pass without a pause of reflection on this brief memorial of the three
brothers, recorded ere Fortune had so widely
separated their lots. The one was now a
lonely old man, tabooed, as I understood, by
society ; another, from some cause yet unknown to me, had stopped short in the
midst of a high and most successful professional career, and had allowed inferior companions to distance him in the race,—nay, as
it appeared to me, had fallen out of the lists
altogether ; while my father, to whom the
paths of ease and respectability scemed
most congenial, was a quiet English farmer,
or squire, should that term be more acceptable to his ears. An "S. F." (indeed, a tiny
" S. F." had endeavoured to insert itself

amid the aforementioned Round Robin, as it
were to complete the family group) I assumed
to be the work of my aunt, Sophia Featherstone, already referred to in my father's
letter, laid before the reader in a previous
chapter, though evidently done before her
marriage with Captain De Vere; and, accordingly, farther on I discovered an "S. F." and
an " A. De V." enclosed within a true lover's
knot, executed, doubtless, during that period
of courtship which was about to lead to but
a few short years of married life. Under-
neath this, I found inscribed (unmistakeably
at a very much later period) a " C. De V."
—the work, I could not doubt, of their only
child, my cousin Constance, now an inmate
of Ravensdale House—and executed as a
slight filial tribute. An " M. F." I was
unable to attribute to any member of our
family known by name to me—unless, indeed,
it appertained to a son of Sir Digges, who,
I was given to understand, had followed in
the evil courses of his father, but whom, of
late, I had lost all trace; and all I could
connect with a certain "L. F." which figured

not seldom on the walls, was that my uncle
Allen Featherstone had a son named Leslie
—his only one now; but, at present, and for
some years past (so far my information
reached), absent from the paternal roof.
Both of these latter initials were, from their
appearance, comparatively recent inscriptions.

I was the more piqued to learn something
more explicit of this last name, inasmuch as
I discovered it in close, and, apparently, in-
tentional, proximity with that of my cousin
Constance; and was endeavouring to draw
some clue from a comparison of workmanship, style, etc., when my attention was
called off by a still more startling discovery;
namely, this signature, " L. F." in evident
connection with the initials "R. E." observed
by me on the brace of pocket-pistols in the
cave of my strange host of the preceding
night.   But here all conjecture was at present
vain.

The sun, too, informed me that day was
speeding, while thus I endeavoured, from
these slight data, to put together the family

history; and, tearing myself away from their contemplation, I resumed my way toward the house.

Pursuing my course through the meadow-flats, I came out on the road; and, presently, found myself opposite a pair of tall iron leaves of a gate—both open, and attached to two granite columns serving as gate-posts. The avenue into which this gateway led had little to recommend it, and the reader may be spared its description. Enough, that it conducted me in time to the gravel-sweep before the house already mentioned, without my meeting any human being to give me in-formation, or oppose my progress.

CHAPTER X.

THE hall-door was ajar, and, in the open doorway, stood the only living creature which I had yet met—if not to give me information, apparently to bar my entrance. This was a raven, of unusually large size, and, sooth to say, of seemingly unusually morose and unfriendly disposition. The creature eyed me for a moment with looks of rising hostility, and evinced a strong inclination to do battle: eventually, however, he appeared to think better of it; and, turning tail, limped — literally limped, for it was slightly lame—into the house, though not without a show of some dignity. I was about to raise the knocker, when my ear caught the sound of approaching footsteps,

and, in another moment, a tall, though
slightly stooping figure—that of the owner, I
could have no doubt, of Ravensdale House—
stood before me.

My first impression, in gazing on this
figure, was, that I had rarely before stood in
the presence of a more remarkable-looking
person. He was considerably over six feet
in stature, and, notwithstanding his stoop, still
looked a singularly tall man—moulded with
considerable symmetry, and even grace of
limb. Certain indications there were—*reminiscences*, I might say, of my father—to be
traced both in form and feature, but I could
scarcely refrain from a smile (certainly not
directed against the individual before me) as
my eye took them in. Were it possible to
suppose that the almost dapper figure of my
parent, and his comely indolent face (not un-
suggestive of good living), could elevate, or
improve, themselves into more grand—I had
well-nigh written more heroic—proportions,
I might, in such case, believe that I was now
gazing on the form which they would take.
My parent—Heaven forgive the filial impiety!

was as unlike a warrior as any pale sub or
dumpy major in the King's commission. The
figure before me would have made no mean
model for a Cincinnatus retired to his farm,
or a Coriolanus, suppliant in Volscian halls.
True, again, my parent still wore his hya-
cinthine locks untinged by time, or what
remained of them, for the topmost crown
already gave indications of baldness. My
uncle's hair, on the contrary, while betraying
no such signs of deserting its owner, had
become of a uniform grey, verging almost
on whiteness. Yet, notwithstanding such
and sundry other differences, I could not
doubt that these were the Featherstone
features I gazed upon, even as I had made
their acquaintance beneath the paternal roof,
though, in the instance before me, they
seemed ennobled by natural talent, by a more
severe course of mental training, and, I could
not help also inferring, by suffering.

On the whole, it was difficult to help feeling
a certain predisposition in favour of the
person who now stood before me. From
first appearances, it was not so evident that

this feeling was reciprocated towards myself. No hand was put forth to grasp mine—no welcome sounded in my ears. Indeed, the first words I heard were :—

" So !—a Featherstone. Your father—if he had little else—was wont to possess punctuality, young man. Are we to charge the tide or a town frolic with your detention ? "

The period, certainly, was one in which the intercourse between elders and juniors was conducted on principles, more severe on one part, and deferential on the other, than those which now obtain. Yet this reception I could not help regarding as somewhat in extreme of the mode—and, in sooth, trying my powers of countenance to their fullest extent. However, I endeavoured to put the best face on it I could, as I replied :—

" Neither tide nor town, uncle, is in fault. Our vessel, it is true, was a few minutes late for the coach, but you must blame the mountain mist for my delay of a day and a night."

I had now entered the doorway, and my uncle preceded me into a small room on the right hand of the hall, which might be either a breakfast-parlour or a study. Here, a young girl—perhaps I should say a young woman—who had been employed in sewing, advanced to meet me with great cordiality, and apparent pleasure, and placed both her hands in mine. Our near relationship was, doubtless, sufficient explanation — if the movement needed explanation — for this frankness of manner; but it appeared to me that it was done partly also as an *amende*, or counterbalance to the absence of warmth evinced in my uncle's reception.

This young person—my cousin Constance, I could have little doubt, though our common uncle made no attempt to enact master of the ceremonies—was tall, and slightly made. Notwithstanding the prominent part which she had taken—and continued to take—in my reception, her manner appeared naturally retiring, almost shy. When speaking, indeed, her features became lit up with animation and intelligence; though, in repose, they had a tendency to assume a more serious, I might almost say a sad, expression;

relieved, however, from all insipidity by an
air of kindliness which they still preserved
under all circumstances. The colour of her
hair and eyes must have been borrowed from
the De Vere, or paternal side; for the fine
chestnut of the one, and the hazel of the
other, seemed to possess little in common
with the darker hues which predominated in
our family. Similarly, too, that markedness
of feature so characteristic of our side, and
which, sooth to say, was scarcely sufficiently
toned down even among the female portion
(so I judged, at least, from some family
portraits quietly slumbering in a lumber-
room at Woodlands), was here replaced by a
more feminine softness.

" I think you mentioned, Constance," said
my uncle, "that your cousin's travelling-
bag had been brought from the village?"

" *Sent* for, uncle: truth compels me to say
that it has not yet made its appearance—
though Dan has been absent some hours
now. However, we know that it had arrived
there in safety yesterday evening."

" We dine at six," proceeded my uncle.

"Your cousin will give you something to stay your appetite until then. In the meantime, I will leave you to grow better acquainted over it. Doubtless, after your journey, you would prefer to keep the house for the remainder of the day; Dan and the travelling-bag shall be my care." And so saying, my uncle stalked from the room, and I was left with my cousin.

"Did I not hear you speak of the mountain mist?" said the latter, as, in conjunction with a neat-handed Phillis, in the shape of a young country girl, pretty and demure-looking, and, doubtless, supplying the place of the dilatory Dan—she placed some refreshments before me.

"Yes, Miss De Vere; you heard, I am ashamed to say, a true confession of my first and awkward attempt to explore your country."

"Indeed — *Mr.* Featherstone" (with a strong stress on the Mr.—and a sweet smile: my cousin, I found, could smile sweetly).

"Well—Constance — Cousin Constance, then."

"Better—very much better, Cousin Frank: I am *determined,* you see, that we shall become old acquaintances, all at once. And now, when you have helped yourself—we lunched an hour ago—let me hear about the mist. Our uncle may appear a little cold at first, but that will wear away ; I doubt not he will offer you some explanation on Featherstone matters ; besides, at present, Dan's protracted absence has somewhat put him out. But now for your travels."

"In a word, then—I lost my way in endeavouring to reach Ravensdale House yesterday, and, but for a very extraordinary character whom I met in my wanderings, would have had to pass the night on the heath." And I attempted a slight sketch of my late host.

"Why, cousin, you have really met the Wicklow Outlaw."

"And who, pray, may this Wicklow Outlaw be?"

"His name, I can inform you, is Michael Dwyer—scarcely, I fear me, sufficiently romance-sounding to grace the pages of a

sentimental novel; and—like our patron
saint—'he comes of decent people:' though
neither numbering any 'gentlemen' among
them, nor are their patrimonial lands to be
surveyed from any steeple I am aware of."

" He boasts himself a peasant, and the son
of a peasant."

" And with truth, I believe. His father,
I have heard, was a small farmer; and, in
this country—so great is the desire for the
possession of land—it is not very easy to
distinguish such a person from a mere peasant, or *vice-versâ*. However, it is beyond
all doubt that he was a quiet, peaceably disposed subject of his Majesty, and reared—
with the exception of Michael—a loyal, in-
dustrious family. Indeed, one of his sons, I
believe, now follows the deplorably common-
place occupation of a car-driver in Dublin;
so that any expectations you may have entertained of making a hero of the Wicklow
Outlaw" (with a certain malicious twinkle
of the eye: had my fair cousin heard aught
of my literary propensities?) "are, I fear,
doomed to disappointment."

" Nevertheless—and notwithstanding this death of my hopes—I still desire to know something more of my strange entertainer."

" And shall, if you will attend on your-self: even when Dan returns, I may not, with certainty, promise you the benefit of his professional services—we sometimes find Ballybay inconveniently near, and its houses of entertainment possess further the repu-tation of being supplied by a certain Mr. Paudeen Gow, supposed to be unequalled in these parts for his deep insight into the mysteries of mountain-dew distillation."

" I have heard of the gentleman," I re-marked, as my eye involuntarily watered at the recollection of the superior potency of his manufacture.

" And," (with another malicious twinkle) " if I am to judge by the neglect of my white-currant liqueur, cousin, you have fallen into the popular opinion. To begin, then, at the beginning. You are, of course, aware of the unhappy insurrection, or rebellion, which broke out in this country about five years ago. We then had a town-house in Dublin,

and lived almost entirely there, since our
uncle was obliged to be in daily professional
attendance at the Law Courts: so that we
were spared the worst scenes of that short
but lamentable period. Michael Dwyer,
however, was one of those who were ' out' at
that time; and when, in the autumn of '98,
all the peasantry implicated surrendered
their arms, and were generally allowed to
return to their ordinary avocations, this man
—whether his acts had been of a more marked
character, or he distrusted the expectation
of obtaining pardon—refused to surrender,
and took to the mountains; where he has
since remained."

" Drawing his chief revenues, doubtless,
from plunder?"

" No ; report speaks to the contrary.
The peasantry (and in this country, you
must know, the mere fact of incurring Government enmity is quite sufficient to enlist
sympathy on your side) contribute liberally
to his support, though his skill as a fowler
renders him in great measure independent of
aid."

"Of *that*, I can bear testimony myself. When I met him yesterday evening, his game-bag was quite full; and, during the short journey he took with me this morning to put me on the right track, he managed to fill it again. Indeed, gratitude, if not a sense of justice, demands I should state that, neither in manner nor conversation, did he give me the idea of a mere robber : I cannot even exalt my hero into a Rob Roy, or a Dick Turpin."

"Such also has been the impression produced on others who have had interviews with this strange man. At the same time, many lawless acts are laid to his charge— committed chiefly, I believe, with a view of keeping the whole of this mountainous range of country in his possession. Some time ago, the Government were desirous of placing these regions more under military protection, and, for that purpose, caused a barrack to be built at the opening of a peculiarly wild valley, some miles from Ravensdale. The contractor had completed the building, and, I believe, transferred it to the proper autho-

rities; but, on the night before the forces
were to take possession, it was blown up by
gunpowder, and remains a blackened ruin to
the present time.   This act has been univer-
sally attributed to the Outlaw."

" These very ruins we passed this morning—and his manner, certainly, afforded no
disavowal of the act.   I am almost inclined
to dispute your verdict of the non-romance-
giving qualities of my hero.   What say you
to an effective chapter describing the blow-
ing-up? of course we should make it a castle,
or, at least, the baronial residence of some
ruthless minion of the Government—and if
we roasted a few Sassenach followers in the
flames, success would be all the more certain.
My only fear is that our Public would annex
the fatal verdict ' improbable ' to the statement that a veritable Outlaw, in this nine-
teenth century, continued, for five years, to
set the Government at defiance, within actual
sight of the second city of the empire."

" That, doubtless, would require to be
modified in the narrative—yet the scene of
your plot, you must allow, is altogether in

your favour, where improbability is to be dealt with. There are few things, I have been told, which your countrymen are not prepared to believe of us—confess, cousin, that you yourself are somewhat disappointed —two whole days in Ireland—and not a broken head (after your Scalp adventure, I may not say a wounded heart) to show for it yet!"

"A poor result, certainly," was my reply, in answer to the young lady's raillery— "more especially to a literary knight-errant in search of incident—after making up his mind to be challenged to mortal combat, or, at the very least, to be invited to tread on the tail of somebody's coat. Is this person (in the dearth of material, you see how entirely I am driven back on my Outlaw) supposed to be alone, then?"

"Such is the belief—at present. Up to some time ago, he had a companion, one Douglas by name—the Dark Douglas, I have heard him called—a Presbyterian from our Black North, and a deserter from one of the royal regiments at the period of the Rebellion.

Our north and south seldom blend together;
and, moreover, this Douglas, I have heard,
was a peculiarly morose and gloomy person.
Nevertheless (and it is regarded as proof of
the influence which this man has obtained
over his followers), even in the extremity of
danger, as was the case in this instance, his
last effort, one as dreadful as it was striking.
was put forth to preserve the life of his leader.
If Dan were here, you should have the tale
with all the embellishments which Irish eloquence—under the further inspiration of Mr.
Paudeen Gow—can throw into it; for this man
is indeed regarded in the light of a hero by
the peasantry of the district. But if you have
patience to listen to a more plain version—
unless, indeed, you would prefer to survey
our limited domains——"

"The Outlaw, by all means. In the interim,
I shall be recruiting strength for our royal
procession. There is a glorious old orchard,
which I must entreat a half hour for—*you* have
not sat for two years on a high stool in a
cobweb-hung office in Chancery Lane, and,
perhaps, know not my anticipations of 'the

country' and all that appertains thereto.
And, if the boat I saw may be trusted to, we
might take the water, while I append my
humble and degenerate name to the purely
Celtic family-scroll which I passed on my
way here."

" The boat is better than it looks. But—if
I might venture to suggest—a quiet *tête-à-tête*
with our uncle would be more suitable
for this evening after your late fatigue.
On the morrow you can show how you can
pull an oar; and, if you can handle a spade,
so much the better—doubtless, you have
also observed how vainly I have endeavoured
to contend with the encroaching inroads of
clover, trefoil, and the too indigenous sham-
rock, on my own peculiar principality. But
now for the Dark Douglas and my short
sketch—*story* you must not expect. The
account runs that this Dwyer and his companion or follower, which I know not, being
belated, had asked a night's lodging at the
house of a peasant or small farmer, ignorant
of their persons. A neighbouring detach-
ment of military, which had for some period

been in pursuit of them, received intelligence
of this by some means or other, and by day-
break the house was completely surrounded
by a Scotch regiment under a Colonel Mac-
donald. This being successfully accomplished,
the Colonel, or one of his officers, advanced
to the door, and commanded their surrender.
In a few moments he was answered by the
Outlaw himself from within. His words, as I
have heard them, were—' Unknown to this
family, we asked of them shelter for the night.
Until they are beyond the reach of danger,
we cannot discuss any terms of surrender.'
Perhaps I should here tell you (as these
words of the Outlaw, it has been alleged,
bore reference to the circumstance), that on
the occasion of this man's refusal to throw
himself on the clemency of the Government,
with the other insurgents, on the termination
of the Rebellion, his father and his whole
family were placed in gaol, on the plea of
harbouring Dwyer, and their few acres,
uncropped and unable to yield any rent,
passed from their hands. (These were terrible
times, cousin; and the long-suffering of our

peasantry, and all sense of justice on the
part of the Royalists, seemed alike to have
deserted the land.) However this may be,
the declaration now made by Dwyer was not
unacceptable to the military leader, since the
probability of sacrificing innocent life in an
attack on the house had been his chief
difficulty. It was therefore answered from
without, that the family would be allowed to
depart unmolested to the nearest place of
shelter ; which permission was at once acted
upon. When the peasant and his family had
left the house, the Outlaw appeared for a
moment in the open doorway, and addressed
the commander of the troops in these words—
' Colonel, you asked us what we intended to
do. *Now* we are prepared to tell you. We
intend to fight until we die.' And immediately the door was closed again. A
regular siege was now laid to the house, and
a fire of musketry maintained on either side,
whenever a combatant become visible. After
a contest of this nature, protracted far into
the morning, the soldiers succeeded in setting
fire to a pile of turf within the building ;

and soon after the whole house was wrapped
in flames. The door—so the soldiers report
the occurrence—was now flung open to its
widest extent from within, and the figure of
the Dark Douglas appeared in the open
doorway, as it were with the purpose of
making a sally. Immediately all the soldiers
stationed on that side of the house, wholly
unsuspicious of the desperate trick, levelled
their muskets and fired, some shots evidently taking effect; and Douglas falling
prostrate on the floor, in front of the
rising flames. Dwyer was defending the
opposite side of the house; but his companion was now seen by those soldiers who
had just discharged their firearms to raise
himself again on his arm, and to address the
Outlaw in these words—' Run for it now,
Dwyer, before the red coats reload, if you
would not die like a singed rat;' and again
he measured his length on the floor. Attracted by the voice, or by the discharge of
musketry, or perhaps by both, the Outlaw
was now seen to come forward to where his
companion lay; and a glance seemed to

place him in possession of the exact condition
of affairs. For a moment he stood irresolute,
gazing on the soldiery, some of whom were
reloading, while others were hastening round
to the other side of the building to acquaint
their companions, whose muskets were still
undischarged. Then he seized Douglas in
his arms; and, with a single bound, he
sprung through the open doorway, while
the whole burning pile fell in with a loud
crash. He slipped, and fell with his burden
on some ice before the door (it was winter-
time) ; but no soldier had his gun ready, and
he was up again in a moment, and continued
on his flight. A tall Highlander, I have
heard, whose heels moved more quickly than
his head, started in pursuit of him ; and it
was partly owing to this circumstance that
the Outlaw effected his escape, thus heavily
weighted ; for he permitted his pursuer to
come so near him as to actually cover, and
protect him, by his person ; and, though the
military who were in the rear of the building
had time to come in front, they saw that they
could aim at the Outlaw only through their

comrade. Dwyer's only memento of this
occurrence was a severe wound in the hand,
marks of which, I am told, he bears to the
present day. His companion was never again
seen in these mountain regions; though
whether he was quite dead ere the Outlaw
carried him from the building, or he subse-
quently expired under his care, or, indeed,
recovered sufficiently to be removed from the
country, is known only to himself. The
peasantry who tell the tale add that he
breathed his last in the Outlaw's mountain
retreat, and that he was buried by his own
hands in one of the neighbouring glens,
where his ghost may be seen, on occasions, to
the present day; but, as no one will affirm
that he himself has seen it, or any appearance
bearing resemblance to the Dark Douglas,
since that morning, I will not ask you to
credit this portion. So ends my tale.—And
here comes old Sable," said Miss De Vere,
as she concluded her narrative, and the raven,
which I had previously observed, stalked into
the room, "to warn us that the dinner-hour
draws nigh."

"What a singular janitor!" I remarked.
"He stood in the open doorway, as I
approached the house, and appeared
strongly inclined to contest my entrance—Is
he, then, old?"

"Not old for a raven, I believe—in fact, a
mere youth; though I have heard our uncle
say that he himself was little more than a
school-boy when he and his brothers domesticated—or, rather, attempted to domesticate
—the creature. This district, or townland
—perhaps you are not aware—originally
rejoiced in the name of Glen-na-Fiac, of
which Ravensdale, I am told (I am no Celtic
scholar), is an English translation; and was
greatly infested by these birds. Our uncle
and his brothers, in some boyish freak,
entered on a campaign to destroy these
creatures; which they carried out, with the
single exception of your unamiable opponent
—then, I believe, a mere fledgling, and
which still bears traces, as you may perceive,
of this war of extermination. Whether it is
owing to an originally morose disposition,
or a recollection of these family wrongs, he

has ever since been remarkable for the same
unsocial, silent (he has not even the recom-
mendation of talking) qualities which he has
evinced toward you.   Indeed, I think, his
especial animosity is directed against the
Featherstone race — not even excepting
myself, who have striven hard to atone for
the cruel vicissitudes of himself and his
relatives.   But there goes Dan's first bell—
rung with a more steady hand than I could
have expected; and, save on company days
(somewhat rare ones at Ravensdale : *you*,
you know, are a Featherstone), our uncle
allows but a quarter of an hour till dinner."

CHAPTER XI.

O N descending to the dining-room, where the inmates were already seated, —the formal drawing-room ten minutes having either expired, or being on this occasion dispensed with,—I was formally introduced to Miss Macklewaine, an elderly maiden relative of Miss De Vere's deceased father, and who completed the company at Ravensdale House. The dilatory Dan (I had already found my travelling-bag safe in my room) was at his post; and (bating an irrepressible loquacity, and one or two *gaucheries*, chiefly directed—if I may so say —against Miss Macklewaine) "got through the dinner," as, I was told, he afterwards expressed himself, "in flyin' colours." My

uncle was somewhat more communicative (a
fact which seemed to restore no little confidence and an accession of cheerfulness to
the mind of my cousin), and, with an occasional absence of manner, played the part of
host with ease and dignity.

"It afforded me much pleasure," said Miss
De Vere, as I rejoined her in the drawing-
room, after a sparing after-dinner libation,
under the equally sparing direction of my
host, "to behold my guardian much of his
old self, this evening. You are to love our
uncle, cousin, as he deserves to be loved—
that is, much."

"To hear—is to obey," was my reply;
"at least (pardon the ungallant condition)
until your commands assume much more
formidable proportions; for, I will confess
to you, notwithstanding some apparent cold-
ness of manner, I felt almost strangely drawn
toward my uncle from our first interview."
I had taken a seat beside my cousin—Miss
Macklewaine, in a distant portion of the
room, having wholly resigned herself to the
influence of the drowsy god. After a pause,

and some reflection with myself, I continued: "And now, fair cousin, that we have touched upon the subject by this chance allusion, forgive me if I dwell for one moment longer upon it—my pardon will be all the more generous act of yours, inasmuch as I see that I already alarm you. Once and for all, then—my uncle—was it at his request that I am an inmate of Ravensdale House? One or two trifling circumstances—the somewhat ambiguous wording of my father's letter to me, our first interview just mentioned, and a chance allusion or two which have since dropped—have led me to the frame of mind which propounds this question. Reply, or not, cousin, as you please; only, do not suppose me so degenerate a Featherstone as to be possessed of that littleness of mind which seeks to assert its position by rendering its owner ridiculous; you, I understand, were the writer of the letter which brought me to Ravensdale House; and here I shall remain as long as I am permitted, and as long as you and my father, for your own sufficient reasons, deem advisable."

I found myself embarked on a longer speech than I had originally intended—nay, *intention* I had none, until my cousin's words suggested an opportunity which might never again occur—or, occurring at a later period of my stay, might be taken advantage of with even a less grace than at present. And I had proceeded, partly with a view of covering this ungracious position in which I was now placing myself—that of a guest who doubts his welcome; and, partly, in order to allow Miss De Vere time for reply.

Alarm I certainly had caused her. Her lip slightly trembled, and she kept her eyes fixed for a moment on the carpet at her foot. Presently, she summoned courage to speak—

"If I said 'yes,' Cousin Frank, 'it *was* by his request,' I would say truly. But so explicit a demand as yours needs an equally explicit explanation; which you shall have. There are circumstances" (and here the mouth quivered again) "which I am unable, and dare not, enter upon: *their* explanation I must leave for clearer heads and stouter hearts than mine: I trust—indeed, I expect

—that you shall not have to wait long. But, on your present question, I am willing to throw all the light that I possess. Most strange and unmerited misfortunes " (and here my cousin's fine eyes filled with tears) " have now—your father writes that you are but slightly acquainted with the family history of late——"

" Say—not at all, cousin."

" Be it, not at all. Such, indeed, is the tenor of his letter. Most strange and un-merited misfortunes have now, for some years, made sport of my dear uncle's happi-ness. You do not—few ever can—know the true nobility which he has exhibited under them. But we all understand the tendency of one fixed idea, preying uninterruptedly on mind and intellect—I am alone, or almost alone, with him (Aunt Ursula is old—indeed, she is my grand-aunt)—with no one to apply to for advice or assistance, should any emergency——"

" Gracious Heavens ! Miss De Vere—you have not—you surely do not entertain any fears on the score of my uncle's reason——!"

"No—oh, scarcely that—and, yet, what inexpressible consolation would it afford me to behold his thoughts turned into some new channel; or, even, obtaining some help in the one in which they now move! To unravel each thread of that tangled web (which I must leave himself to lay before you) seems now to have become the one purpose of his life. Need I tell you with what risks this is accompanied, under the lonely life which we lead here, with so little to tempt the mind to other occupations? And, accordingly— or it may have been my own fears—I have remarked, of late, an increase of eccentricity —we are, Frank" (with a faint attempt at a smile), "accounted an eccentric family; and a certain irritability—a new feature in *his* case—causing me such serious alarm that, after much thought with myself, I asked his permission to write to your father, and invite him to Ravensdale. At first, he refused; chiefly on the score that your father had once disapproved of certain acts of his, and that little sympathy was to be expected between them in consequence. On a second, and more successful, attempt of mine, he gave his permission—partly perhaps to relieve my anxiety; partly, I almost feared (though no allusion to the subject was made by either of us), from forebodings of the same nature as my own. I worded my letter with great caution, so great—it is now plain from your father's deputing you, Master Frank—that I failed to convey any adequate conception of the feelings under which I wrote: but, indeed, my only object was to bring a near relative to our uncle's side, leaving him to dispose of the rest as he might think proper. On receiving your father's reply, announcing your near arrival, 1 at once laid it before him, and could not fail to see that the change of visitors afforded him pleasure—I might almost say relief. Doubtless, the disapproval of the course of conduct which our uncle had pursued still rankled in his mind—and your own pro-fessional studies will render you a more congenial companion: to say nothing of the legal knowledge which you have obtained, and which cannot fail to be of assistance."

I endeavoured to receive this last intimation with becoming gravity: *my* legal knowledge, save the mark! would find ample room in the silver thimble which my cousin had again resumed, having laid aside her sewing on hearing the question which had brought about this conversation. The further to preserve my judicial dignity, I added, "But is—or was not—my uncle an eminent barrister, himself?"

"Assuredly. But—not to say that two legal heads should be better than one—professional men, I have heard, like other opinion than their own, or, at least, *with* their own, in matters deeply personal to themselves.

"And now, my dear Frank," said my cousin, holding out her hand to me—"now that I have solved your difficulty as to your position in Ravensdale House in a manner which ought fairly to be satisfactory to your feelings, let me express the great—the very great gratification which it affords me to see you an inmate here. To night I will have to thank you—nay, let me now thank you—for a repose to which I have been for some time a stranger. But Aunt Ursula has opened her eyes, which is a sign that she expects her tea; while here comes uncle to challenge you to an encounter at chess."

After some games of chess (by great good fortune, I managed to come off conqueror in one or two: though I had made but few moves until I found myself in the hands of a master), my uncle asked me a few questions concerning his brother, my father, and our Gloucestershire life; after which, the conversation reverted to my own university and law studies. He put to me one or two legal queries—incidentally, and, as I judged, without any present intention of following them up: and, sooth to say, *here* the jade Fortune deserted me altogether—for, answering at random, I found, by subsequent reflection, that my answers had been wholly incorrect.

On the whole, on reviewing my day's experience, I found it a somewhat strange medley of disappointment and pleasure: of disappointment, at not acquitting myself better in the presence of my uncle—possibly, too, at sight of the scene of neglect, I might almost say of desolation, which reigned around : of pleasure, in the society of Miss De Vere, and in the counterbalancing footing —of coadjutor and protector—on which I seemed to be received by her. And, in such a frame of mind, I sought my room for the night.

But whatever repose I might be instrumental in giving to other inhabitants of Ravensdale House, I was certainly sparing in reserving a sufficient stock of that article for myself; for, spite of my wanderings, it was some hours after I had retired before I could succeed in banishing the waking thoughts of the day from my mind—in which the tall, picturesque form of my uncle (already invested with an air of mystery)—and the deep, truthful eyes of my cousin played conspicuous parts. Nay, when, at length, I passed into the world of dreams, like visions still pursued me—mingled, indeed, with the more sharp ferrety orbs of Miss Macklewaine, and the rich Milesian accents—*the* richest I

had yet heard—of the bibulous Dan. Nor,
when the veritable Dan himself announced,
in the same accents, that it was time for me
to arise, and deposited the hot water for
shaving at my bedside, was it without
difficulty I succeeded in persuading myself
that he was not again offering his apologies
for the soup which he had deposited on the
ancient brocade of the latter lady.

CHAPTER XII.

" THE orchard, I think you said, was to be
your first introduction to the Ravensdale territories?" was Miss De Vere's inquiry,
as, some hours after breakfast—spent by
her, I was given to understand, in household
duties, and by me in the library—we issued
together from the house.

" The orchard first, by all means—though
the boat, the summer-house, and these much-
enduring flower-beds (if you have sufficient
faith in my qualifications as a landscape-
gardener) have all their special attractions."

"You are forgetting Old Martha—a new
Featherstone at the Big House, and not
making his first visit to Martha! I think we
had better be content with the orchard to-

day, as through it lies our way to the cottage
—and be sure you say you came *straight*
through it."

" And who is Martha ? "

" Martha has rocked the cradles of—I
dare not say how many generations of Featherstones. Prepare your filial ears to hear
your father spoken of as 'Masther Dominick'
—and, under the title of 'the Colleen,' be
pleased to understand that reference is intended to your humble servant. Nay, even
the awful Sir Digges, the great head of our
house, does not escape being classed as one
of 'the young gentlemen.' "

" Colleen means, I believe, little girl ? "

" Precisely; and I, who am, or ought to
be, a discreet, elderly person, was once that
little girl. I should not wonder to find you
pass in her eyes as a mere *gossoon* (you know,
cousin, I have the advantage of you in point
of years)—in fact, unless you can succeed in
throwing something venerable into your face
and manner, a merely promising baby."

" If this old woman," said I—perhaps, not
over well-pleased at the allusion to a really

nominal disparity between the ages of myself and the fair girl who walked by my side
—" is an old retainer of the family, why (I
ask that I may not appear a complete igno-
ramus before such a depository of family
lore) has she not followed the fortunes of the
great Sir Digges himself?"

"Partly because, for sundry crimes and
misdemeanours, she has, in her own *parlance*,
'given the back of her hand to him' (which,
rendered into your London vernacular, would
stand, I suppose, that she has 'cut' him)—
and partly because old Martha—whom, I
perceive, you are already prepared to dis-
like—clings, like the cats (though indeed
honest Rover"—addressing a large New-
foundland dog which gambolled by her side
—"would more nearly represent her family
attachments) to the soil. Doubtless, you
are aware that Ravensdale House was *the*
seat, before the Featherstones boasted a
Baronet at their head—though, perhaps,
more broad acres than Sir Digges and our
uncle here can now muster between them at
present. When Castle Coote brought with

it this title into the family, Ravensdale
House was made the patrimony of the second son."

"Then, Sir Digges once held Ravensdale
House?"

"No; not exactly. That is, he never
came into actual seizure and possession,—
which is, I believe, the proper phrase among
you gentlemen of the long robe. Norman
Featherstone, his father—and our grand-
father—then lived ; and was, of course, the
holder of Ravensdale House. Him, our
uncle Digges would in the ordinary course
of nature (am I correct, again?)—succeed ;
while our uncle Allen here—to whom neither
house nor lands appertained, nor appeared
likely to appertain, only a slender second
son's portion—embraced the profession of
the law. On the death, however, of old Sir
Percy (a distant relative) it was found by his
will that the eldest son of Norman Featherstone could choose between Castle Coote
and Ravensdale House—the rejected estate
reverting to the second son; and uncle
Digges accepted Castle Coote, as the better

of the two—I have heard our uncles say that
Norman Featherstone somewhat 'dipped' the
family acres.   In accordance with these conditions, and by a process of 'cutting off'
somebody or something—which, I confess,
takes me a little out of my legal depths—our
uncle Allen succeeded to the Valley of the
Ravens on the death of his father."

" The whole matter was, then, an amicable
arrangement?"

" Perfectly so, Mr. Cross-questioner.   I
have frequently heard all the brothers speak of
it as a sound and equitable distribution of
the family property, made in strict accordance
with the wishes of the testator; and they
continued to meet on most cordial terms for
many years afterwards—so that I fear your
hopes are small of founding a legal reputa ·
tion on any re-opening of it.—But here we
are at Martha's door."

After passing through the orchard, and
making our exit by a postern door, our
course had lain, during the preceding conversation, through, or beneath, " the melancholy shade of boughs," formed by a lower

forest of pines, which here made a considerable turn toward the rear of the Big House;
and, beyond this, lay the cottage or cabin, to
which we had been directing our steps. It
stood on the outskirts of the present Ravensdale bounds (truth to state, of no very
extended proportions); and, but for its
greater neatness, differed little from the
ordinary peasants' cabins of the district. It
must, however, in fairness, be stated that
these cabins presented a marked contrast to
the wretched hovels which I had met in the
course of my wanderings of the two previous
days—habitations, if they deserved the name,
which had too closely corresponded with the
scene around them. Here, however, the
very cabins or cottages might be said to
smile with the surrounding landscape.

The half-open door (that is, a door consisting of an upper and lower compartment,
one ordinarily open, the other closed) conducted on to a hard earthen floor, swept
and scrupulously clean. At one end of the
apartment lay a large nook or recess, used
as the hearth, and on which the usual peat

sods smouldered. Reared against the wall, and glistening white by lavish application of freestone, was "the dresser," an essential ornament of the reception-room of every Irish cabin, whose owner can command it. On the shelves of this was arranged, and conspicuously displayed for further ornamentation, the entire service of delf, tinware, glass (a limited supply—a broken piece or two of looking-glass included), and cheap chimney-piece baubles, which the establishment boasted of, flanked, on either side, by a mug or tin porringer, containing a nosegay of fresh-gathered woodland flowers. Some wooden stools and a small table—all bearing similar evidences of freestone—were arranged about; and a wooden stand—similar to the huge candlestick I had observed in the cave of the Outlaw—stood by the wall, ready for evening use; though, instead of the bog-deal there used, I remarked that it bore a rush-light, which then, and for years after, supplied the place of the ordinary " dip," even in the kitchens of the gentry of the more remote country districts. A few highly-coloured prints with scriptural subjects, and a ballad setting forth the loves and misfortunes of Willie Reilly and his dear Colleen Bawn, were affixed to the walls, and completed the entire equipment of the apartment. Ceiling there was none, and the bare rafters and thatch of the roof—both now dyed a deep ebony by the turf smoke—were the sole covering between the inmates and the sky. A pot, filled with potatoes, and suspended over the hearth by means similar to those observed by me on the previous occasion just referred to, was now bubbling, and proclaimed the noon-day dinner near at hand, if, indeed, the extreme anxiety of a fine fat pig outside the half-door as we entered, and his piteous tones of expostulation at the slow movement of time, had not already apprised us of that fact. On one of the white and well-scoured stools, sat old Martha herself—solacing *her* delay with a short black pipe—her only indulgence, I was given to understand. A snow-white cap set off a face which must have been comely in its time, and was still intelligent; and an equally clean

apron imparted an air of neatness and
tidiness—not, I grieve to say, to be found
generally among the peasantry of other districts of the island : for Martha, I could perceive, was essentially a peasant woman, and
not by any means so old as I had been led to
expect. Indeed—as I afterwards learned—
she was a contemporary, or very little more,
and foster-sister of my father and uncles;
and her phrases of " Masther Dominick,"
" Masther Allen," and " the young ladies
and gentlemen " in general at the Big
House, did not so much mark any superiority
of years on her part as traces of the tone of
conversation which prevailed around her
during her residence there. Taken from the
peasant's cabin to be an humble companion
and assistant to these aforementioned young
ladies, she had straightway relapsed into her
former state and status as soon as family
changes and arrangements made her services
no longer necessary within the walls of the
Big House. While, therefore, it was but
reasonable to suppose that she had derived
benefits, in habits and training, during her

sojourn with "the family," she might, on
the other hand, in many respects be accepted
as a specimen—a favourable one, doubtless
—of the better-ordered and more intelligent
members of the class inhabiting the happier
portion of Ireland, and raised beyond the
pressure of immediate want. With the paid
professional domestic she had nothing whatever in common, while she afforded repeated
indication that no association with "the
quality" had, in the least, subverted those
national characteristics common to the Irish
peasantry.

"I have brought you a visitor, Martha,"
said Miss De Vere, as we now found our way
into the cottage—having, with some in-
genuity, evaded the entrance of the fat pig
with us—"I suppose, I need not add—a
Featherstone."

"Eh! Miss Constance—an' isn't it good
for sore eyes to see a young gentleman about
the place, as it used to be in the old times.
It's well I remember the Captain (he'll be his
father)—the fine young jintleman that came
down to see the lone woman, in his goold

lace, and cocked hat, and ilegant regimentals, before he went to the wars. I'll go bail you often heard Masther Dominick tell of ould Martha ? "

My memory was, I confess, somewhat treacherous on the subject ; but, providentially, I could call to mind—or did call to mind, Heaven help me!—a certain pound of tobacco, with which I represented myself as entrusted (so, at least, I made effort to say, though a roguish look in my fair cousin's eyes somewhat marred the effect) for her sole and separate use.

"Ah ! there now," said the highly-pleased old lady, "that's more than ever I got from Castle Coote ; misfortune came with it into the family."

"Oh ! Martha," broke in Miss De Vere, " you are unjust ; Sir Digges never omitted his inquiries for you, whenever he came to Ravensdale ; and even visited you."

"Ay—ay," said Martha, in that indescribable tone with which alone the Irish peasantry permit themselves to express a doubt, or rather difference of opinion, with their

superiors in station. "It's little he thought
of the lone woman after his back was turned.
That wasn't the way with the poor ould
Masther up at the House, that stuck to ould
Martha through sorra an' throuble—oh wirra
strue! that ever they came upon the house
an' dacent family."

"But, you know, Martha, you were asked
to live at Castle Coote."

"*Me* to live at Castle Coote!" exclaimed
the highly-incensed old woman,—"me to
live with flauntin' hussies an' tinselled
draggletails—me that was reared up with
the young ladies themselves, and among
respectable women."

"Well, well," said Miss De Vere, now
truly pained, and anxious, if possible, to
check the tide of eloquence which was
plainly rising to the lips of Martha, "all
that is changed now."

But Martha's eloquence was not to be
checked; or, at all events, it merely transferred its current into the new channel thus
suggested.

"Changed! ay, ay, sorra on it for change!

it was never good for the family—changed!
thrue for you, alanna, a change it was to
see such a Lady Featherstone. *Lady* Featherstone!'' (with a strong accent expressive of scorn), '' one of them same draggletails, only oulder and deeper—a housekeeper,
she called herself.''

'' I must ask you to cease this subject,
Martha,'' now interposed Miss De Vere,
with some severity in look and tone, '' I did
not bring my cousin to see you for such a
purpose. It is very well known that the
present Lady Featherstone *was* a housekeeper
at Castle Coote (and a respectable person
for her position)—that is all that can be
alleged against her, if, indeed, it is a crime.
On the other hand, it is, I believe, allowed
that she has effected an entire alteration in
the domestic regulations of the Castle.''

'' The divil a doubt of it!'' broke from
the incorrigible Martha. '' ' Bundle and go,'
was the tune, when Nancy Bell found herself
one of the quality.''

The words and manner, however, of my
cousin had, in reality, brought the old

woman to a stricter sense of propriety, her
last remark being the farewell shot of the
vanquished. Not but, at intervals, a drop-
ping fire—certain mutterings, which, to alter
the metaphor, bore no very distant resemblance to those of a dog which had been
checked for flying at "a suspicious character,"
were still to be heard, in which " changed!"
and "Lady Featherstone" were alone distinguishable.

" I am sorry, Frank," said Miss De Vere,
turning to me with some appearance of
embarrassment, "that your first visit to
Martha has not been made more agreeable
to you. I trust it will not happen again."

" No, Miss—no, Miss Constance," said
the half-contrite Martha ; " I'd sooner bite
my tongue off than offend you, or the poor
Masther. But I get ould, alanna : and age
and crossness goes together. Come and see
the ould woman again, Masther Frank. It's
often the Captain, your father, and all the
young gentlemen used to ccme down, to
smoke their pipes, and reddy* their guns

* Ready, *i.e.*, put in readiness.

and fishing-rods, wid, maybe, a half-bottle
from the dining-table for ould Larry—-my
husband was alive then, Masther Frank; I'm
a lone woman, now, and it's not long I'll
throuble anyone."

Somewhat mollified, my cousin promised
that our visit should be repeated shortly,
and we left the cottage—to the evident relief
of the fat pig, who had beheld (by standing
on his hind legs, like a dog, and looking
into the cabin) the dinner preparations
wholly suspended during our presence.

CHAPTER XIII.

RAVENSDALE HOUSE.

IT will be unnecessary for me to weary the reader's patience by entering into any minute details of the few succeeding weeks, as passed by me at Ravensdale House. Of my uncle, I saw but little; and was thrown, by consequence, more into the society of Miss De Vere for company—a circumstance which, perhaps, I was not disposed to find fault with, at the time. As some compensation for his absence, excused on the plea of business, he had, however, at an early period, introduced me into, and made me free of, the library—a large and not uncomfortable room, sufficiently removed from the sitting-rooms to insure perfect quiet. As

might be naturally expected, the legal ele-
ment was largely represented on its shelves;
though miscellaneous literature, and that of
a fairly recent character, was by no means
lost sight of. Whatever might be the nature
of my uncle's avocations, they seldom brought
him to this room. When he did enter it
while I was there, it was generally but to
take a volume from the shelf, consult it for
some time, replace it, and then glide from
the apartment again. If his manner at
times, on such occasions, gave me an impression that he was about to enter on more
confidential terms with me, I was as frequently doomed to disappointment. Sometimes, it is true, he approached the part of
the room where I was sitting; inquired into
the nature of my studies; and, with great
clearness, and a perfect *grasp* of the subject,
elucidated any difficulty which had presented
itself to me. This was, of course, more
apparent in matters connected with his
profession (my father had suggested to me
the desirableness of keeping up an acquaintance with my legal studies), but there were

few branches of a polite education on which I did not find him competent to give able and enlarged views.

Smarting under a sense of the poor exhibition of myself which I had made before him on my first evening at Ravensdale House, I took the earliest opportunity, really from no other motive, to consult some of the standard works on the luckless subject of my break-down ; and it so fell out that my uncle entered the library, and approached my chair, as I was thus employed. Contrary, however, to my expectations, a shade of displeasure passed over his face as his eye glanced on the open page, and, with some reference to a volume he was in search of, he passed on. After that, he continued as heretofore, though perhaps more seldom, to assist my studies by commenting on some favourite topic connected with them ; but all subjects bearing on himself or our family entered no longer into our conversation. On these, my cousin's words had led me to expect some important explanation from him : this, I could not help concluding, he had now deferred, if not wholly

abandoned ; nor was I free from a certain feeling that I myself was the unconscious cause.

My out-of-door pursuits were sufficiently
diversified. The neighbourhood abounded
with game, and there was no lack of fowling-
pieces, wholly disused, it is true, for some
years, but readily brought by me into order
again. The surrounding streams, too, were
plentifully stocked with excellent trout, and
Dan, an enthusiast in all sports by field and
flood, not only made me acquainted with
the several flies at which these speckled
denizens rose, but also diligently sought, far
and wide, for the hare's ear; the cock,
grouse, and woodcock hackles; the lark's,
starling's, and wild duck's wing ; the wren's
tail, the pig's bristles, the badger's hair, the
hog's down ; with furs of the fox, otter,
marten, and water-rat—in a word, the various materials which go to the composition
of the artificial fly. I possessed some knowledge of fly-tying; and, with a little care
and labour, was not long in providing myself with a " book " of these ingenious
little make-believes.

During my operation of preparing my book of artificial flies, I had opportunities of beholding the mode of life at Ravensdale House, passing, as it were, in review before me. It is true, my occupation confined me for several hours each day to my own room (for a current of air, the sudden opening of a door, or window, would have scattered all Dan's hard-sought treasures to the winds)— where Master Sable, the morose raven I have already referred to, was my solitary visitor. But, even from this place of seclusion, I could gain a pretty accurate idea of the daily routine.

It was a favourite pastime of this " gentleman in black " to climb, by slow and tedious labour, a tall sapling which grew under my window, and which brought him on a level with my apartment—for he was unable to raise himself from the ground by means of his wings; though, once on an eminence, he could manage a short and safe flight back to terra-firma. Nothing could well be conceived less social or companion-like than our interviews on such occasions. The creature sat

on a bough, or perched on the window-stool,
sometimes even on the table near me (owing
to the heat of the weather, I was obliged to
leave my window open), and contemplated
both me and my work with hard, indifferent-
seeming eye, wholly heedless of any attention paid to him. Indeed, I could have
believed him unconscious of my presence
altogether but for the alacrity with which he
took advantage of my slightest absence.
Once, I caught him in the act of walking off
with a precious packet of otter's fur—procured for me by the adventurous Dan at the
cost of some wet and sleepless nights, and
no small expenditure of Mr. Paudeen Gow's
distillation—and, with considerable difficulty,
regained possession of it. On another occasion, a paper of fishing-hooks (*that*, I had
almost a mind to leave him to satisfy his
curiosity upon, were it not that, setting aside
all considerations of humanity, my uncle
appeared to set considerable store by the
the brute) was the object of his desire.
When he grew tired of contemplating my
operations, he either descended, or, climbing

still higher up the tree, clambered on to the roof of the house, and was lost to sight for that day at least—amid leads, gutters, and gable-ends.

I cannot better conclude this chapter than by giving a description of the internal arrangements, as far as I came to be acquainted with them, of this strange pile of building : for strange it certainly was fast becoming in my eyes. More especially as told they must be, if I am to render the further course of my narrative intelligible to the reader.

From foregoing conversations, already inserted in their proper places, the reader, doubtless, will, by this time, be acquainted with the fact that Ravensdale House was the original ancestral seat of the Featherstone family, under its old Celtic title of Glen-na-Fiac, prior to the Castle Coote accession under the will of Sir Percy. It had been built at a period when the family acres extended much more widely over the surrounding district than at the time of which I write. Thus the various relics of ornamentation (which—

to compare small things with great—gave it some distant resemblance to those long-buried cities of Central America which the traveller comes across—now in the midst of the wild forest, and, anon, overrun by the brake and the thicket) had all been the works of generations long past; but indifferently cared by later ones; and now, latest of all, left wholly to the weak hands of my cousin, with such assistance as could be occasionally obtained from the erratic Dan, and an aged gardener named Tim, who regarded the orchard as his sole and only charge. At every step, therefore, it was no unusual circumstance to find the carved stone-work of gate-pier, parapet, or portico scattered— and submerged—amid the luxuriant meadow; or ignobly fulfilling the office of stop-gap to some rent in hedge, or boundary wall. The family acres having dwindled to their present limited number, and—so it might be fairly inferred—my uncle's whole revenue being derived from their circumscribed area, every spot was turned to purposes of utility, and the merely ornamental grounds of a past era were obliged to conform to the new order of things as best they could.

The house, built wholly irrespective of its present limited number of inhabitants, was chiefly composed of two wings, extending equally on either side of the main entrance. The eastern, or right-hand wing, was now the only inhabited portion (the arrangement to concentrate the inmates might be one of comfort and economy; and the space was ample). While the western wing, lying on the other side of the entrance-hall, was never used—beyond the limits of a couple of stiff and cold reception-rooms, most seldom required—for any purpose whatever. These vast solitudes lay entirely open, but were never intruded upon by the inmates: as for the domestics of the establishment, *they* were seldom to be found singly, beyond their proper regions, after dark.—It was rare, at the period of which I write—I believe it is rare still—to find a country-house in Ireland (with any pretensions to age) which did not possess its varied traditions of fact and fiction : wherein deeds of wildness, violence,

and extreme prodigality alternated with tales
of ghost, goblin, and haunted chamber,
which they had left behind them. In such,
Ravensdale House was peculiarly rich. The
matters of fact were numerous, and, I believe,
beyond dispute—but the credibility of
the several ghostly or spiritual legends
which they had brought in their train, I must
leave to the taste of the reader to dispose of
as he may see fit. It may be that he is a
devout believer in ghostland, and I should
only incur his disapprobation by appearing
to treat the matter in a light and frivolous
manner; or, he may scout all idea of such
visitations, and censure me for devoting any
portion of my pages to so foundationless a
subject. I shall, therefore, content myself by
stating that, while the whole of the domestics, with Dan unmistakeably at their head—
who was as arrant a coward as ever it has
been my lot to meet—were all unanimous in
asserting the house to be "haunted," I
myself never came across anything which
was not explainable—eventually, at least—on
material and natural grounds.

I have a clear recollection of my first exploration of these silent solitudes.

I chose a bright and sunny day (not to affect a fortitude with the reader greater than he may be disposed to credit me with) for my visit; lest, by any means, some portion hidden in deeper gloom, the wind moaning down some chimney, or the slamming of doors, might lend appearance to those tales of the kitchen and pantry with which I was already amply stored.

I had been poring over a volume in the library, and, meeting with some difficulty on which I was desirous to have the elucidation of my uncle—at the time superintending some field operations—before proceeding with the subject, I had closed my book, and strolled into the sitting-room. There, Miss Macklewaine informed me that my cousin, with her attendant maidens, was deep in the progress of "a churning," and would not be disengaged for some time. Miss Macklewaine was not at any period a very enlivening companion; and, somewhat disappointed— half hours with my cousin had come to be

looked forward to by me not without interest
—I betook myself out again on the first convenient opportunity; and now found myself
standing in the entrance-hall without well
knowing how to dispose of my time. The
door on the left-hand side of the hall stood
ajar—and I entered.

It opened, as I was already aware, on the
first of the large reception-rooms previously
mentioned—the other lying behind it, and
connected with it by a pair of folding-doors.
A few loungers were scattered through the
room, and a number of stiff, old-fashioned
chairs were arranged round the walls. Whole
generations of Featherstones stared at me
from out their equally stiff, old-fashioned
frames; while a cold, empty grate added—
though it *was* summer—to the cheerless
appearance of the apartment. I had already
been in this and the adjoining room, and
there was little in them to further tempt
curiosity; but, opposite to the door by which
I had entered, was another, which communicated, I had no doubt, with the whole of the
unoccupied wing—and the spirit of inquiry

being strong upon me, I turned the handle, and passed through.

I now found myself in a very much larger room, and looking, perhaps, even larger still by reason of its almost complete emptiness. A single table—now bearing nothing save a thick coating of dust—ran down the centre of the apartment; and a few chairs and a sideboard—all with similar covering— were the only other articles of furniture. The floor was uncarpeted, but consisted of darkstained oak, bearing trace—where the dust permitted—of the high polish to which it had been subjected. I could have little doubt that this had been the banquet-room of former times; and my imagination pictured to me the oceans of claret, the mounds of solid food, and the correspondingly large supplies of whiskey-punch which it had been the means of dispensing to the inmates and their friends. On the right hand, as I entered, was a large window, opening on the front of the house; and, opposite to this, on the other side of the room, was another door—to which I now directed my steps.

This door conducted me out on a landing, from which *one* flight of stairs descended—I could not doubt to the lower regions; while a similar one *ascended*, and led, as I conjectured, to the remaining portion of the wing : the whole, balusters, steps, and landing being covered with a still deeper coating of dust than that which I had observed in the banquet-room. Choosing, in the first instance, the descending flight of steps, I soon arrived at their termination, and found myself—as well as the very imperfect light informed me—in a long arched gallery. The stone flagging, the damp appearance of the walls, together with the distance I had descended, led me to conjecture that I had now reached the ground or basement portion of the building; and the nature of the various compartments which opened off, on the right hand and the left, furnished an additional reason for my supposition. Most of these, indeed, were pitch dark, while a few were but faintly lighted by small, low windows, firmly secured by iron bars from without, and thickly coated with a mass of cobwebs and dust from within.

In fact, the only light—besides that which
struggled to find its way down the flight of
stairs—came from these latter means of
communication with the outer world. Within
some of these receptacles—caverns they now
appeared—formed in the solid stone-work,
lay vast mounds of saw-dust, damp and
blackened by time and moisture; and I had
little doubt that they once contained the
claret and other wines, for use in the neighbouring banquet-hall. Others still contained
a few articles of coarse furniture, and, doubtless, had been set apart in past generations
for use by the host of domestics and humbler
followers which a large and sporting Irish
family of the period usually maintained. No
sound broke the stillness of these half-sub-
terranean regions; and it was evident that
they had been wholly uninhabited for some
considerable time. It was with something
approaching to relief that I retraced my steps
through them, and, ascending the flight of
stairs, found myself again in the comparative
light of the landing. My curiosity, however,
was by no means allayed, and I now con-

tinued my course upwards, by means of the second or ascending flight.

These steps, in their turn, led to a corridor, off which a number of sleeping-rooms opened—such, at least, I conjectured them to be from their size and situation, though now perfectly empty. The doors of most of these stood ajar; and, finding nothing in them calculated to raise or satisfy curiosity, I was about to abandon my examination of them when a single closed door arrested my attention. Here was *some* difference, at least; and I turned the handle. The door, however, refused to open, and further trial led me to discover that it was locked. Had I then at length reached the Bluebeard's closet of Ravensdale House—the veritable haunted chamber, which had served for the nursery of so many wild legends and goblin tales? I attempted to look through the keyhole, but nothing save the most pitchy darkness met my gaze. I put my shoulder to the door, but it refused to yield. I was about to abandon the attempt and pass on, when a key, depending from a hook on the

wall, caught my attention, and I had no
sooner turned it in the lock than I found
that the door yielded to my efforts. A slight
rustling noise was audible, as I cautiously
opened the door ; but the darkness rendered
all alike invisible.   In a moment, it had
ceased ; and I advanced into the chamber.

A faint streak of light (invisible, I could
now perceive, from the door) enabled me to
see in which direction the window lay, and I
had no difficulty in opening the shutters.
The apartment, I thereby found, occupied
an angle of the house, and looked out partly
into the court-yard.   I now turned toward
the room itself.   It was, like the others, a
sleeping-room ; but—contrary to them—still
contained the whole of its furniture, intact,
as far as I could judge.   A small bedstead
stood opposite to the window; a chest of
drawers and toilet-stand took up the better
part of one wall ; and a round table occupied
the centre of the apartment.   I could have
almost believed that the room was still in
use (by my uncle, when he sought more
complete retirement;   or   by   one   of   the

domestics—only, indeed, the furniture and general appointments were of a superior order for that latter supposition) were it not for the dust and cobwebs, which must have been the accumulation of some years. The white counterpane on the bed bore its own portion of coating; the table and chest of drawers might, in extreme emergency, have supplied the place of writing-tablets; and the seats of a couple of chairs could have served for the same purpose.

Without some clue, all conjectures were vain on my part as to the history of this chamber—for a history, I had already established with myself, it possessed; and when I had gazed upon all that was to be seen, and carefully closed the shutters, I retired from the apartment.

At the end of the corridor, a much more narrow staircase ascended yet higher. On mounting it, I found myself directly under the roof of the whole pile. A few skylights, scattered here and there—further assisted by some chinks in the roof—dimly revealed the machinery of beam, rafter, and coupling, by which the roof itself was sustained; but, saving a greater accumulation of dust and cobwebs than I had yet witnessed, there was nothing else visible. My object in exploring to this latter extent was in close connexion with a tale which had obtained more than ordinary credence among the domestics of the house, and had been told to me by the bibulous Dan in extenuation of some absurd piece of cowardice on his part. It was to the effect that a former butler, under a former Featherstone, had here committed suicide by hanging himself to a certain beam, which—in proof of the tale—I should find in a certain portion of these aerial regions; while, as a further assurance, I was to discover the floor under the beam stained with marks of blood. What connexion there was between hanging and blood-letting, I was not informed. Dan —who was never to be caught in a corner— suggested that the unfortunate knight of the napkin might have fallen down in the act, or that those who discovered him had opened a vein in the hope of restoring him to life— " there's many ways of accountin' for it,

Masther Frank " (by this time I was generally recognised as Master Frank throughout the household), " wance a man's willin' to give in to it." The foregoing, however, was the morsel of fact—if fact it was ; the fiction to which it had given origin will readily suggest itself to the mind of the reader, gifted with ordinary powers of imagination :—as, that he was still to be heard (and seen by sufficiently daring eyes), walking up and down these stairs—serving ghostly dinners in the banquet hall—drawing the daily consumption of claret from the empty wine-cellars—with the like. Beams and cross-joists there were plenty—and more than one fulfilling the necessary conditions. But of stain or bloodmark I saw no trace—though the imperfect light and accumulated dust might sufficiently explain this.

Having thus satisfied my curiosity—as far as an actual inspection of these regions of silence and desolation permitted—I now turned my back upon them, and regained the entrance-hall without any difficulty. My cousin was still engaged in her household duties; and, as the day was now too far advanced for a fishing or shooting excursion, there was nothing else for it but to resume my studies in the library. With which intention, I had actually opened the lately discarded volume in the hope that chance might bring a fresh accession of light to its pages, when I became, for the first time, aware that a small gold pencil-case, the parting gift of my mother, with which I occasionally took notes in the course of my reading, was no longer in my possession. I had used it during the morning—indeed, some notes which I had taken by help of it were now before me; and I could also distinctly bring to mind that I held it in my hand when starting on my tour of exploration. Few inducements—as well as few opportunities —could arise for my laying it aside in those empty rooms; and the mysterious chamber —I had already come to regard it as such— at once occurred to me as the first place where I was at all likely to do so. Yes; I had it all quite clear in my memory now. In my efforts to unfasten the bar which held the shutters of the window in that room, I had laid it—so I could perfectly call to mind —on the round table—nor had I any recollection of taking it up, when retiring.

Closing my book, I left the library, and hastily retraced my way through the entrance-hall, reception-room, and larger room lying beyond it. They were still as silent as the grave. In a few moments more, I had opened the door and shutters of the chamber already referred to. But the table before me was perfectly empty. I examined the floor carefully, on the supposition that the missing article might have rolled off the table; but with no better result. I even did so much violence to my own clear recollection of the matter as to prolong my search through the dust-covered attics; but no trace rewarded my efforts. I had carefully locked the door after my first examination of the furnished room; and I had now found it to all appearances as I had left it. The intrusion of a domestic into any portion of the wing was an event, of all, to be the least expected; while I had every reason to believe that the various members of the family were otherwise occupied.

Puzzled with myself, and with these desolate-looking, and yet seemingly not deserted regions, I again turned my back upon them for the last time. All idea of ghostly agency I entirely scouted. But, whatever reasons had previously existed for attaching a mysterious character to the furnished chamber—in my dearth of information I knew it by no other name—they were by no means removed by this latest occurrence.

CHAPTER XIV.

I T has, I make no doubt, been already remarked, by some previous writer, that the inevitable consequence of two persons of opposite sex dwelling under the same roof—young, occupied by no previous attachment, not absolutely repelling in form or mind, nor coming within the prohibited degrees—is that one, or both, should fall into the toils of the tender passion. I may, also, put forward, in further extenuation of any present weakness of mine which the more acute reader may have detected in this direction, that the terms on which I met, and enjoyed the society of, Miss De Vere, were peculiarly dangerous in themselves. From our first interview, I had been openly regarded by her

as protector and guardian of the house of
Ravensdale, bringing repose of mind to herself, and destined, perhaps, in time (though
how I was yet to learn) to obtain a like
mental tranquillity for our common uncle—
a position, I need scarcely say, by no means
slightly flattering to a very young man. I
possessed, moreover, frequent opportunities
of beholding the amiable disposition and
truthful air of my relative, openly laid before
me in all the confidence of friendship and
family ties—further enhanced by good looks,
lady-like manners, and accomplishments
which might lay fair claim to being considered extensive, without being superficial.
I am sure I have only to add that all these
attractions were heightened by a certain
tinge of melancholy (apparently superinduced
over a naturally sprightly disposition), to
render any further explanation of mine need-
less to the more romance-loving reader.
I may not deny that, for some time, visions
of a fair creature holding out a delicately-
gloved hand, in lieu of words which refused
to come, did occasionally appear before my

mental vision, waking and sleeping. But,
gradually, the lovely apparition grew fainter
and fainter—and, about this period of my
narrative, the image of my cousin began
wholly to supply the place of it. No one,
possibly, so I reasoned with myself (and
being employed upon a somewhat old subject,
it will not be expected of me to hit on any
very new or original views upon it)—no one
marries his, or her, first love; and, the
emotion having found life—if I may so speak
—during my mountain adventure just alluded
to, it now seemed as if it had wholly taken
the direction of Miss De Vere for its object.
A young man of twenty may be excused if,
for some time, he does not perfectly know his
own mind; but, now that this preparatory
period had passed, I could have little doubt
that the pleasure I found in my cousin's
society—the desire to convert that settled
sadness into a more sprightly frame of mind,
and the impulse to do something which would
write me "man" in her estimation—had,
one and all, their origin in that passion which
has furnished so inexhaustible a theme to
poet and romance-writer.

I have already mentioned that I had begun
by degrees to resume my legal studies—with
the assistance of my uncle's library, and the
occasional aid which he himself afforded me
in any passing difficulty. The opportunity,
indeed, was a most excellent one for bringing
these studies to a successful termination (had
my father any views of this nature in sug-
gesting to me to become an inmate of
Ravensdale House?)—I had already eaten
the number of London Temple dinners which
the wisdom of our legal authorities has pre-
scribed to Irish students; while my present
distance from Dublin by no means precluded
me from keeping the remainder of my terms
there. I could scarcely hope for a more able,
and, indeed, willing preceptor than my uncle;
and the retired life we were now leading
afforded ample opportunity for reading.
These thoughts—I leave the aforesaid
romance-loving reader to divine their origin
and prompting cause—having, for some
time, busied themselves in my mind, a more
steady and regular course of study had now
become the result.

" My father," was my remark to my cousin, " cannot be expected to do much more for me than to put me on the high road to a profession—every young man, whose means are not quite inexhaustible, ought to have a profession."

" Most true, Frank," was Miss De Vere's reply; " how hard is the lot of those who are obliged to turn from such a road! Nay" (and here something approaching to a sigh escaped from my relative)—" nay, equally hard is it to be debarred even entrance on the path."

The latter allusion, I could have no doubt, bore reference to the Leslie Featherstone aforementioned (as the reference which preceded it was to his father, my present host), who, as I had been given to understand, discontinued his university studies when leaving his native shores. With my mind, however, more particularly dwelling on the single incident—whatever might be its cause —of my uncle's retirement and seclusion at Ravensdale House, I had hitherto felt no sufficient inducement to do violence to the evident reluctance with which Miss De Vere approached family matters, by inquiring into the subject. Leslie's departure, too—I had learned—had been prior to that circumstance, and afforded no explanation of it whatever. I saw no reason, however, why, on the present occasion, a sigh should accompany this reference to the matter.

"But such a lot, thank Heaven!" continued my cousin, after a moment's pause, "is not yours, Frank. There can be little doubt that our uncle will entirely approve of such a course, and render it all the assistance in his power."

"Will not Miss De Vere add her own approval?"

"My approval, Frank! My dearest wishes, would surely be the more appropriate expression ; which are yours, most heartily. My approbation, I fear, would be as presumptuous as my assistance, were I to offer to place *that* at your disposal."

"Fair lady's approval has incited men to even higher deeds ere now, Constance."

"Oh ! surely, Frank. How dull I have

been this morning ! Have we, then, been
placing to the credit of ambition—a sense of
duty—the desire to gratify your relatives,
what turns out to be but a skilfully-directed
shaft from the Blind Bow-boy himself?
But who am poor I to stand proxy for with
my smiles (be sure they shall be sincere ones,)
—the lady of the runaway horses?—or has
Master Cupid been yet earlier in the field
with you?"

"Neither she of the runaway horses, nor
an earlier——Is it, then, so improbable an
event that I should bring a whole heart to
Ravensdale House?"

"Perhaps not, Frank," said Miss De Vere,
whose manner now betrayed some slight
alarm—"pardon me if I have hurt you by a
contrary supposition. Of—of whom, then,
do you speak?"

"Of *whom*, Constance! Is my love, then,
so unlooked-for that I must declare it even
more plainly?"

I spoke, perhaps, scarcely with the suavity
which the occasion demands. If I could
not accuse my cousin of dulness, at least I

looked sooner for some responsive sign, were it but the eloquence of silence. True it is, her breath now came more quickly, while her face, which a deep blush had at first suffused, as soon changed to more than its former paleness. But the gaze which she directed towards me, so far from bespeaking the coy or tender maiden, was rather that of one who felt (and yet hesitates to trust the senses) a sharp and unexpected wound from a quarter whence it was least to be looked for. Such, at least, was the interpretation which, shortly afterwards, under more sober reflection, I put upon it. *Now*, however, carried away by the tide of my own eloquence, once I had opened the flood-gates (after the manner, I believe, of very young men on such occasions), I was proceeding—

" Yes, Constance—dear Constance, if I may so call you—can you not believe it is you of whom I speak? your image, which has incited me thus to make a name and position for myself, under the hope that yourself may yet share them with me—? "

" You must not," here broke in my cousin,

—"you must not, indeed, Frank, proceed any longer in such strain. I did not—believe me, I *could* not have expected this. You recurred so often to your late adventure —to the fair creature whom you had rescued, that I imagined—indeed, we all imagined—your thoughts to lie wholly in that direction. Confess, cousin—relieve me by confessing—that it *was* so ? "

" Is everything, then, to be more worthy of credence than that I should learn to lift my eyes to Miss De Vere ?   Granted be it (since so it pleases you) that I have recurred to the series of incidents which accompanied my journey here—granted, I dwelt more particularly on my meeting with Lord Killgrove and his daughter ; I had not then met Miss De Vere. You, Constance, were wholly unknown to me save by name, and by a description far short of mere justice. Is it not as fair to suppose that my thoughts were occupied by Lord Killgrove himself and what has been achieved by *him*, as by the image of his daughter, and a love, which would be truly founded on first sight; and *that* a very short and confused one?"

"Be it so, Frank. On me rest the charge of associating my cousin with the fair Miss Warden—I had, at least, the example of all knight-errantry for my precedent. *Yours*, then, was the less romantic incentive of professional advancement. Must I no longer suppose the union of the two permissible— even in my land of day-dreams and air-built castles? Lord Killgrove was once John Warden (I have heard our uncle speak of him a hundred times), and climbed the ladder from humbler rounds. To woman's wit all appears possible, if—if——"

"If I too commence my ascent of the ladder with somewhat of the like application—I read your thoughts, Constance."

"You do—and truly, Frank. Such words do indeed give expression to hopes—dreams, I have now called them, which your own narrative (returned to perhaps oftener than you yourself are aware) has given rise to. Pardon me if, to myself, I have indulged in visions of a happiness for you, Frank, which

has been denied to your less fortunate kins-
folk."

"And yet, no sooner do I set about the
task—this ladder which I am to climb—than
you yourself withdraw from me the only
prize which is now valuable in my eyes."
And, so saying, I closed—somewhat melo-
dramatically, perhaps—the volume which
had hitherto lain open before me. "Am
I to be permitted to learn, Miss De Vere,
what reasons cause my addresses to appear
so peculiarly distasteful to you?"

"Distasteful, Frank? They come so
wholly unexpectedly upon me, that I can
scarcely analyze my feelings. *Reasons* there
are innumerable—apply what epithet to
them you please—what if I plead—was ever
my sex driven to such defence! what if I
plead (since reason you demand) our disparity of years?"

"You jest, Constance—we are both of
an age; so registry and relatives agree."

"But both should not be of an age—such
advantage as years render (is it not better
we should pass from such seriousness to

jest?) should be yours—the husband's possession. Enough! you reckon years by the
mere days they number—such have not been
mine. My years of dull repining—already
they count to me as ages—are not the preparation for the cheerful and lightsome
companion you are to look for. Just now,
you spoke of reward—I must smile when
next my glass returns to me the faded,
spiritless thing which was to tempt you to
such forensic eminences! May it be your
lot—nay, I am sure it will be—to secure a
more fresh, a more fortunate prize. I have
long since dedicated my life to our uncle's
service—for that alone am I now fitted."

"In a word, you have no longer a heart
to give, Constance?—let me believe *that*, at
least, if you would not leave my vanity
without all solace?"

"Believe what you will, so it free us
from this most painful and embarrassing
position. Only tell me you are—you will
be again, the dear friend and companion
who was to aid me in restoring peace and
tranquillity to this house of mourning."

She held out her hand. The tears, which had, for some time, stood in her eyes, now fairly broke their barriers, and streamed down her face; and she turned to leave the room. Her hand was already on the door, when she again addressed me—

"I cannot trust to this parting. Will you not give me some hope—some assurance upon which I may rely?"

"That my thoughts shall cease to turn to you, Constance?"

"Save as a friend—as a brother should, if you will. I cannot—indeed, I dare not—now seek to extricate myself from the net of snares and perplexities which have grown around me:

'Oh, what a tangled web we weave,
   When first we practise to deceive!'

But believe me, for my own sake—for all our sakes—the explanation shall not be deferred a moment after it is in my power."

I were less than the man I would have written myself did I longer seek hope or encouragement in the looks or language of my cousin, or continue to urge a suit which, beyond all doubt, was the occasion of pain and consternation to her. The impossible is the grave of hope, and such a grave I must be blind indeed not to see opening between myself and the love which I asked. While Miss De Vere's hand was, therefore, on the door, and she stood for a moment irresolute, after uttering these words, I advanced with the best grace I could, and (hard task for a young man) made effort to tone down the ardour of my previous words —or, in other language, to fall out of my love as I had fallen into it; endeavouring, in as intelligible phraseology as I could employ, to reassure, and restore tranquillity to, the trembling and apparently bewildered figure, which received my words in silence.

" I will believe," were my concluding words—and, possibly, all that were sufficiently coherent—" since you have permitted me—that I have been somewhat late in the field, and that your Bow-boy has stolen a march on us in this direction also. Let me lay this flattering unction to my soul—and honour shall dictate the rest. I *will* climb the ladder—though virtue is to be its own reward."

She turned her face toward mine, as if with a view of gaining additional confirmation of my words from its expression, and held out her hand to me. It faintly returned the pressure of mine—doubtless, as a ratification of our treaty. In another moment, I was alone in the library (where our interview had taken place), and had time to ponder over the strange and unexpected scene which a few chance words—for my declaration of love was by no means premeditated—had brought about.

That I had hit upon the true cause of my rejection — a previous attachment — I could have slight doubt, even setting aside the whisperings of vanity. Not only had my expressed surmises in that direction remained uncontradicted by word or gesture, but such allusion seemed to call forth the only maidenly confusion—the only light of love in my cousin's eyes, which had appeared during the course of our interview: at such a moment, the loving heart stood revealed in all

its beauty and unapproachableness. That
Miss De Vere had loved—and still loved—
I set down, therefore, as beyond reasonable
doubt. But did this fact sufficiently explain
the expression of surprise, pain—humilia-
tion (for these—one and all—had appeared
to me to flit across the clear, truthful features
of my cousin) which my words, when first
clearly understood by her, had called forth?
Was it so very surprising that a young man
should address a youthful unmarried woman,
with whom he had been some time domesticated, in the language of love? Were such
accents generally painful to female ears?
Or (and to conclude my brief catechism) *was*
the position of her who heard them rendered
thereby humiliating? Wholly unable to
evolve any further light out of this mystery,
I sat for some hours longer in the library
(under the delusion, I believe, that I was
"reading"), and heard the first bell ring
for dinner, without any clear comprehension
of the meaning of a single line of the volume
which had lain open before me.

On descending to the dining-room, I found

Miss De Vere's chair vacant—for the first time since I had taken up my residence at Ravensdale House. Some inquiry after her health trembled on my tongue, but I had too little confidence in my powers of self-command to give it utterance.

" You lose appetite, and I think your mind is scarcely so clear as it was," said my uncle, who, as ill luck would have it, had started a law topic during the meal—" work, downright hard work, never injured any man—provided one combines it with proper exercise and recreation. We have had no fresh trout these some days ? "

Promising to essay my piscatorial skill on the first opportunity, I made an early escape to the drawing room—half hoping, half fearing to find my cousin presiding over the tea-table. But Miss De Vere was not in the room. A few minutes after I had taken a seat in a recess formed by one of the windows, Miss Macklewaine—to my great amazement —came and sat down beside me. Hitherto, I had looked upon this lady as associated, in some mysterious manner, with meal-time—

and with meal-time only. On the recurrence
of such periodic occasions, she was called,
and took her place at table. But, at all other
times, I found her occupying a comparatively
isolated chair, and, whether asleep, or engaged on a very Penelope's web of needle-
work—demanding, and receiving, little more
attention than the seat on which she sat.
The reader, therefore, will not deem me
guilty of any very violent exaggeration in ex-
pressing my surprise at being thus unexpectedly called upon to conduct a conversation
with this sleeping, sewing, eating, and exceedingly deaf automaton.

"Constance will have had a nice day for
her drive."

"Indeed!" said I; "I was not aware that
Miss De Vere had left the house to-day.
Has her drive fatigued her, then?"

"Yes," replied—or, rather, said—the old
lady (my words had plainly gone for nothing),
"she had promised before you came—an old
schoolfellow of hers—very nice young lady
—lives at the Priory—the great lawyer's
place, you know—extraordinary man!"

" Miss De Vere has, then, gone on a visit ? "

" Oh yes—several times. They make a great deal of Constance. I suppose she told you they had written ? "

" No ; my cousin did mention her former school companion and the inmates of the Priory ; but she spoke not of any present intention of visiting them."

" Ah, probably not," (I had now modulated my voice to the required pitch and distinctness)—" no doubt, she thought you would be lonely—that is, until you are better domesticated. You must come and talk to me every day—your uncle is but poor society."

" We work at the law, you know, together. He gives me considerable assistance, now and then."

" Yes, yes ; I have no doubt. But a strange man—a very strange man." And Miss Macklewaine tapped her forehead in a peculiarly mysterious and meaning manner.

" My uncle has had much to try him, I believe ? "

" Oh, no doubt, no doubt—never was the same man since Leslie went. That was a sad occurrence."

" Very," said I, in lack of better reply.

" But young men will be young men, Master Frank."

" Too true," said I, affecting a look of profound and premature wisdom.

" That they will—that they will," repeated the old lady. " But here comes your uncle for his tea. I have been telling Master Francis, Allen, that he will miss his cousin."

" Ay, ay! we shall all miss Constance. But the run will do her good. She looked pale and nervous to-day when she came to bid me good-bye. She told you when she would be ready to return, Frank ? "

The question was sufficiently embarrassing. My safest course appeared to me to adhere strictly to the terms of it, in making my reply.

" No, indeed, Sir ; she did not."

" Ah ! I also forgot to ask. But we must give her fair breathing-time ; no doubt she will write. In the meantime, hold yourself

in readiness for her escort home from the
Priory. I should like you much to meet
its owner. The man is not *quite* (doubtless,
I shall be considered somewhat hypercritical,
as well as contemptuous of public opinion,)
after my style of a forensic orator—*lawyer*, I
hold him none. But you should know, or at
least see, all styles. His wit (a little coarse,
perhaps, and not always in severe keeping,
but wit certainly,) and his conversational
powers are something wonderful."

"You speak, Sir, of the great Irish advocate—the 'people's advocate,' I believe?"

"Ay, advocate—declaimer, perhaps, would
be still nearer to the mark. His speeches
and addresses are mere harangues—abound-
ing with bad taste, coarse invective, tawdry
ornament, and surprising bursts of genius.
However, at home he acts the host and
entertainer of mind and body to perfection;
and is particularly fond of the society of
young men. He has brought up an amiable
family. Sarah, your cousin's friend, is a
highly interesting young lady."

I had heard—who at the period, and since,

has not ?—of the great national wit, orator, and genius of debate—the future custodian of the Irish Rolls; and, on any other occasion, would have learned with highly-pleasurable curiosity my near probability of thus meeting him on a footing of domestic freedom and equality. Now, however—so great a hold had other affairs taken upon me—I heard the announcement with comparative indifference; or, if curiosity was aroused, it was a curiosity in which my cousin (and the promised means of again finding myself in her presence) partook quite as largely as any of the other present inmates of the great counsellor's well-known suburban residence, not even excepting himself.

When, at night, I made an early retreat to my room, it was more with a view of thinking over the occurrences of the day than of seeking rest. Among the category of marked events, which propel the stripling—by bounds rather than by equable motion—into the state and condition of actual manhood, his first declaration of love has, I

believe, been ever allowed to hold a distin-
guished, if not the foremost place. This mile-
stone of life I had now reached; and with it
had also come my first fall—another, and, I
believe, scarcely less marked event of the way.
Was it to be wondered, then, if I desired to
escape to the solitude of my room to examine
into the nature of the result; to see, to pur-
sue the metaphor a little further, what bones
had been broken, what wounds, bruises, and
contusions I had really received? Such
proceeding, I am sufficiently aware, belongs
more to the *heroine* of Romance; the hero
being supposed to find vent for his feelings
in a series of brilliant and impossible ad-
ventures, in defending the fair fame of his
inamorata against "all comers," while she is
thus employed in her appropriate bower. For
such departure from established course I
have to plead my state of hobbledehoyhood;
which, from time immemorial, being accounted
that of neither a man nor a boy, may absolve
me from the duties of either. Besides, there
were neither rivals nor Rosinantes at Ravensdale House.

It was the first night of moonlight since my arrival; and the round full moon was just rising as I took my seat by the window. Yes—so ran the current of my thoughts—I still loved my cousin: I felt that it was impossible to help loving that earnest, truthful nature. But was it with the love of which I spoke this morning? I was obliged to confess to myself that the words and manner of Miss De Vere had done much to bring about a change in its impassioned character. The least exhibition of coquetry, a moment's hesitation, a semblance of doubt of her own heart, might have converted me into a still more importunate and confirmed wooer. But all such I knew to be foreign to the manner of my cousin. I had been offered the love of a friend—of a sister, as the utmost to which I could look; and, all things considered, I was very much inclined to accept it—and that, too, with the sincerity with which I knew it to be proffered. It is possible, such creatures of inconsistency are we, that I should have required some further time to arrive at this conclusion (during

which time I might also have affected sulki-
ness and a sense of injury), had the unknown
attachment of Miss De Vere appeared to flow
in a more fortunate current. But so largely
leaned the evidence to the contrary—so
little did I behold of the insolence of the
prosperous gale, so much of humility—
deprecation, if I may use so strong a term—
that my defeat remained almost unfelt.
The battle, as it were, had become a drawn
one. And, as the chiefs of opposing forces
are occasionally seen accepting the hand of
fellowship, in lieu of the victory which was
to be the lot of one or other, so it was with
some such feeling of alliance and amity toward
my cousin that I, at length, sought my
pillow. Indeed, it is not beyond the range
of possibility that my thoughts recurred to a
certain fair vision seated in a flying chariot,
though looking anything but Medea-like, ere
I sank into entire unconsciousness.

The night, however, was not to pass over
without an incident bearing on the course of
this narrative. But the details demand a
chapter for themselves.

CHAPTER XV.

WHEN I awoke, I was under the impression that it was the broad light of day which filled my room. Nor was I undeceived until, jumping out of bed and approaching the window, I beheld the round full moon still riding in silent majesty in the midst of the sky, and lighting up the landscape of woodland, and waving meadow, with the Irish Channel beyond : a distant view of which my room commanded. At that period of my existence, with unimpaired digestion, and none of the cares and perplexities which subsequent relations of life bring about with them, it was unusual with me to find my night's rest thus broken in the middle ; and, attributing it to the disturbing events of the preceding day, I was about to again address myself to slumber, when a noise struck on my ear—one, too, which seemed somehow to have a recent and familiar sound about it. Nor could I doubt—after a few moments' reflection, and a recovery of the lost train of ideas which I had when awaking—that it was a similar sound which had interrupted my repose.

The principal staircase lay close to my room door; and I could have no doubt that footsteps were now slowly, and somewhat cautiously, descending it. That such an act, at such an hour, should be essayed on the part of any of the domestics, was a conjecture to be wholly rejected. Nor was Miss Macklewaine much more likely to avail herself of the occasion for a midnight stroll. The Master of Ravensdale himself, therefore, alone remained; and I endeavoured, with increasing interest, to gain, by help of the sounds and the direction which they took, some additional corroboration of such a supposition. Now, they had reached the foot of the staircase—anon, they were proceeding through the entrance-hall, and, in a few moments more, the hall-door was cautiously opened, and as cautiously closed again. My interest—curiosity, if the reader will—was, by this time, so great that I was standing at the window of my room, under the expectation that this midnight excursionist might choose the direction of the eastern wing of the building, and so pass within view. In a few moments, this anticipation was realised. Yes—there was no mistaking that tall, and yet slightly stooping, figure. The features were scarcely distinguishable by the aid of the moon, but the general air and bearing admitted of no doubt. It was indeed Allen Featherstone, who, emerging from the border of shadow cast around the house by its own pile, crossed the open space, and was again lost to sight by the intervening brushwood and evergreens. Previous conversation with my cousin (and, more particularly, her words— " This night, I will have to thank you for a repose to which I have been for some time a stranger ") naturally reverted to my mind; and, as naturally, it invested the occurrence to which I was now a witness with even greater importance in my eyes than present evidence might seem to warrant. To put on some articles of clothing, was the work of a very few moments; but, this accomplished, my course lay no clearer before me. I could not conceal from myself—indeed, more than one circumstance had already brought it more immediately before me—that my uncle had stopped short of his confidence with me, not alone from a consideration of what little assistance I promised to afford him, but, also, from a suspicion that I was sent to Ravensdale chiefly with a view of playing the spy upon his movements. How, then, would it be, if he caught me in the actual and unmistakable fact? On the other hand, I could not but attach importance to those words of my cousin's which I have just repeated. *She* was now absent; while I had voluntarily taken upon myself the office of friend and assistant to her. If any risk or entanglement were likely to attend on such midnight excursions of our common relative, what excuse could I offer to myself or to her, for my abandonment of the post of duty? These opposite considerations coursed through my mind more rapidly than I am now able to give expression to them. The result was that I seized a bough of the sapling which waved within a few inches of my window and swung myself into the tree itself: determined to combine them to the utmost that their conflicting nature permitted—namely, to follow my uncle sufficiently near to ward off any danger which might threaten him ; but, if possible, to escape recognition by him.

Short, however, as the time was, no figure was any longer visible, as, letting myself down from branch to branch, I reached terra-firma, and took my way through the copse, or shrubbery, of laurel and arbutus into which this midnight apparition had disappeared. I was not, however, left wholly without clue. The shrubbery—it formed little more than a narrow belt—was succeeded by the beech-walk, already mentioned in a former chapter of these memoirs. The high wall of the domain ran, in a tolerable state of preservation, parallel with one side of this for its whole distance, and the open domain itself stretched on the other side, sufficiently lit by the broad moonlight to show anyone passing across its surface. I could therefore have little hesitation in concluding that the figure I was in quest of had passed down the beech-walk; and, under such impression, took that direction myself.

The walk—a pretty long one—terminated at a postern door in the domain wall, opening on the public road. It had evidently been constructed for the purpose of enabling foot-passengers to avoid a long détour by way of the principal entrance and avenue, and, as such, had been frequently used by myself. On passing through it, I stood upon the road-side; and was left to mere conjecture in what direction now to steer my course. The person whose steps I was attempting to follow might have turned either to the right hand or to the left, and so passed either up or down the public road.

Nay, rejecting both directions, he might have crossed over the road, and entered the plantation which there stood opposite, forming, as it were, a continuation of the beech walk. Again, however, all clue was not entirely lost to me. The road ran perfectly straight on either side ; and, with the exception of the portion exactly opposite to me, had neither wood, grove, nor coppice to obstruct the view, or hide the traveller. For at least half a mile on either side of me (and no one, unless gifted with seven-league boots, could have accomplished more than that distance in the time which had elapsed since the disappearance of the figure as noticed from my window) the way lay perfectly open to my gaze, sleeping under the calm moonlight. A very much smaller figure could have been· at once detected, if on it ; but the whole distance on either side was now perfectly clear and unobstructed. The weary tramp and wayfarer had long ere this found shelter—it was to be hoped, temporary oblivion from care—under brake, hedge, or haycock, or in more hospitable barn. The early farmer, with his load for the neighbouring fair or market, was not yet astir; while the very beasts of burden of the peasantry—turned out to snatch a meal from the road-side—had either escaped to more plentiful, though forbidden, pastures, or, with a lively sense of the toil of the coming day, were now taking an equally hasty hour's repose. Far as the eye could reach, I saw nothing save the thick coating of summer dust which lay on the road; and I could arrive at one inference only—namely, that had the figure indeed passed through the postern door, it must have crossed over, and entered the plantation. I endeavoured to confirm this by an inspection of the road itself—if haply the dust bore the recent marks of footsteps in that direction. But so many foot passengers, vehicles, and beasts of burden had passed that way on the preceding day—it had been market-day in an adjoining town—that all was alike confused and indistinct. In another moment, I had ascended the green and sloping bank, which here formed the opposite road-side, bedecked

with many a primrose and dewy violet; and
was beneath the leafy covert of the grove,
or plantation.

This grove, running at right angles to
the road, occupied the site of a winding
ridge, or slightly elevated and narrow strip
of land—the country, on each side of it,
remaining flat and untimbered. It could
not be more than a couple of hundred yards
broad (at parts, not even so much), and I
still felt tolerably certain that—on the supposition that the figure had indeed entered
it—it could not emerge into the open country on either side without detection. All,
however, now preserved the stillness of the
grave. The feathered inhabitants of the
woodland had not yet awaked to their daily
avocations. The young and tender boughs
of the fir, pine, and other kindred species
(with which the grove was entirely planted),
drooped heavy with dew, the crystal glo-
bules of which glittered plentifully among
the hair-like foliage peculiar to this class of
tree; and there was not even sufficient wind
to vary the fantastic patterns of moonlight

which were imprinted on the tangle of grass, woodland flower, and brushwood at my feet. At such a period of stillness, it appeared to me that the distant breaking of a branch— the rustling of leaves—the mere motion of a person through the close underwood, should be audible to attentive ears. But no such sound was heard by me.

Taking the centre of the woodland, where the ridge attained to its highest elevation, I advanced cautiously; pausing at intervals to listen, as well as to look out on the open pasture-lands lying on each side. These pasture-lands contained a goodly supply of cattle and sheep, all now collected into groups, and taking some hours' repose before the coming day. Here and there, was scattered a peasant's cabin, cold and smokeless in the broad flood of moonlight; and, anon, the more imposing appearance of a farm-house and haggard. Motion, however, of any sort I saw not.

After proceeding for some time in this direction, the grove terminated. The land became all of the same uniform flatness; and

I found myself—as, of course, my previous rambles led me to expect—within a few yards of the sea-shore. The pasture-land extended to within a short distance of the brink : a narrow margin of rocks intervened; and, laving their base and permeating their hollows and cavities, lay the ocean itself, almost as still as the surrounding elements. The tide, indeed, had been some time in; and the first moment of the ebb was as yet scarcely distinguishable. The farmers and peasantry of the neighbourhood had here constructed a rude boat-haven, by a slight adaptation of the facilities which the configuration of the rocks themselves presented; and a coble or two lay scattered about. On the horizon, a couple of large ships rode at anchor, probably becalmed, and waiting for the morning's breeze to resume their course.

It was not without some hesitation that I had thus advanced from under the shadow of the woodland: from reasons already stated, I had no wish to be detected in my midnight ramble. But, emboldened by my previous impunity, as well as by the

appearance of utter solitude which reigned
around, I now found myself on the brink
of the waters. The great deep heaved and
throbbed at the foot of the rock on which I
stood, nor could I doubt that the time of
its outward departure was just at hand;
but, saving this ripple along the very margin, all on its surface remained motionless
and still. It was, at least, certain that no
one had lately put off from the shore; for,
such was the flood of light poured from the
full moon on the whole expanse of waters,
that the veriest cockle-shell of a boat would
be subject to detection.

A short distance ahead of me, and almost
on the borders of the sea, lay the old parish
church of the district; disused since the
building of a new and central one, and now
a mass of ivy and incipient ruins. In truth,
but for its churchyard—whose use was still
dictated by filial piety—its gates were now
rarely opened. I jumped over the low wall
which separated this enclosure from the surrounding pasture-land; and found myself
among a mass of graves and tombstones of

every imaginable size and variety, interspersed between, and, at times, almost covered by, tall and luxuriant crops of hemlock. A large padlock secured the church door, sufficiently indicating by its rust and stiffness that, of late, it had not been put to much exercise. A little examination now assured me that the churchyard was entirely deserted, and that the same universal stillness presided over it. I could not, indeed, gain access to the church; but all appearances warranted me in inferring that no one had intruded recently on its solitude.

My walk round the sacred edifice brought me to that portion of the burial-ground set apart to the Featherstone family. I had already paid more than one visit, in the course of my rambles, to these memorials of my ancestors. With a single exception, there were none of very late date—that exception being in the case of a son of Sir Digges, whose death was here recorded as having occurred some few years before the period of which I write. I sat down on this more recent tombstone for the purpose of taking a last look around me. Neither sound nor motion was perceivable—if I might except a faint indication from the neighbouring ocean that the ebb was setting in ; and I could have no doubt that I was utterly alone among the dead.

That a certain family history of a mysterious nature attached to the tomb on which I now sat, I was already sufficiently aware. The name of its occupant was rarely mentioned—and never voluntarily : when chance did bring about an allusion, signs of embarrassment and pain were seldom wanting, and either complete silence ensued, or the subject of conversation was at once changed; nay, even the very domestics forbore all reference to the matter. This latter, it is true, I·might have broken though : and with respect to the bibulous Dan, I knew a key which, I had no doubt, would resolve his taciturnity even on this point, if skilfully applied. Hurt, however, by my uncle's suspicions, I had determined to make no move in such direction, and consequently I knew little more than the stone on which I was now sitting recorded. Hitherto, in the course of these memoirs, it has been my object to lay fact and circumstance—affecting my tale— before the reader in the actual order in which they became known to myself—as the most natural to the autobiographical form of narrative, and in accordance with every one's own personal experience. Nor (though, in truth, the remains which now slumbered beneath me, and the history which was associated with them, were still to exercise great and vital influence on the progress of events) is it necessary that I should, at present, make any departure from the rule which I have laid down for my own guidance. I was now on the eve of becoming acquainted with these facts—as far, at least, as lay in the power of my informant—and thus, they may take the place proper to them in the general order of my narrative. On the present occasion, it will be sufficient, therefore, to mention that the memorial slab on which I sat stated that the enclosed remains were those of Marley Featherstone, son of Sir Digges Featherstone (and consequently my cousin)—that he had

been 26 years of age at the time of his
decease—and that his death had taken place
just four years prior to the period of which I
now write.   My previous conjectures (I had
the ill fame of Sir Digges—the complete
silence of my father on the point, to suggest
them) were that he had been the black sheep
—the disgrace of the family, and that he had
here buried his disgrace : and the reader will
learn a few pages farther on that my conjectures were correct.   To infer such a son from
such a father needed no great strain of rea-
soning, even if the silence of my own respectable parent permitted any other solution.
Under what peculiar circumstances his career
was thus cut short I was at the same time to
discover, and the narrative fully cleared up
the taciturnity of the remaining branches of
the family.

Again jumping over the low parapet, and
retracing my way by the sea-shore, I entered
the wood—under the impression (as strong
as the circumstances at my disposal would
permit) that the figure I had seen pass by my
window was either still in the plantation, or

had not entered it at all. Time, however, now pressed. In my hurry, I had left my watch behind me; but I could not doubt that the arrival of the dawn was not very far dis tant: under which, the chances of my detection in returning to the house would momentarily increase. Abandoning, therefore, all intentions of more protracted search, and keeping to the lower parts of the woodland, I made the best of my way towards home, observing, however, a sharp look-out around me, and making as little noise in my progress as the nature of the ground and brushwood permitted.

I had accomplished about half the journey in this manner, when my steps were suddenly brought to a stand-still. I had now reached perhaps the broadest part of the woodland strip, as also the lowest—a depression, in the nature of a valley, or dale, descending from the main ridge at this point. The space before me was partially clear; and a green sward supplied the place of the rank and tangled herbage found in the more thickly-wooded portions of the plantation. This clearing was now empty; but, on its margin, a large tree had fallen—and, seated on the trunk, with his back turned towards me, was, I could not doubt, the object of my search. A few paces more would have brought me quite into the clearing, and a mutual recognition must, of necessity, have followed; but my eye, by chance, had caught a slight movement of the figure, and I now stepped back into the more dense shade. Scarcely had I done so, when my uncle—for no doubt remained on my mind that it was he—arose from his seat, and stood on the borders of the open space. For a moment, he cast a keen and searching look around; and then retired with slow, and indeed, as it appeared to me, lingering step, toward the more thickly-wooded portion. In another moment, his tall figure had disappeared within the foliage in the direction of the house, and I found myself alone.

I allowed sufficient time to elapse after my uncle's departure to guard against any risk of our meeting; during which, I made a hasty examination around me. The clearing, I found, was not far from the boundary wall of the woodland enclosure, with which it was connected by a narrow but well-defined footpath.   This boundary wall—built, doubtless, to preserve the young trees from the incursions of the neighbouring cattle—was crossed by a stile; after which, the footpath pursued its course through the pasture-lands outside, and, to all appearance, in the direction of the small boat-haven I had just visited.   Indeed, I now saw, from the lie of the land, that there was some gain, in the matter of distance, by entering the woodland at this point from the sea-shore, instead of at its termination; and I could not doubt that the path had been used for that purpose.   *Within* the stile, it wended its course through the clearing; and, arriving at its opposite side, proceeded through the wood in the direction of Ravensdale House.   On the whole, it appeared to me that it was available for persons passing from the boat-haven to the public road, as also to the Big House.   Striking into it, I soon discovered that my conjectures were correct. In due time, I crossed the road, and entered the lawn of Ravensdale. Fortunately, the first early streaks of dawn had not yet made their appearance in the sky, as I cautiously raised the sash of the window, and as cautiously closed it again. Dressed as I was, I threw myself upon my bed; and, busied in vain conjectures as to the cause of the unexpected incident of which I had just been a witness, I felt not the approach of sleep until it had gained dominion over me.

CHAPTER XVI.

O N descending to the breakfast-table—
after a plentiful ablution of cool and
refreshing water, with a view to obliterate
all traces of my nocturnal excursion—I
found Miss Macklewaine deep in the perusal of a letter, which, she informed me,
Miss De Vere's escort of the previous evening had brought from her, to notify her safe
arrival.

"Constance and Sarah have the Priory
nearly to themselves. She arrived quite
safely; and has enclosed a note for you."

My cousin's note did little more than
repeat to me, in other words, the substance
of Miss Macklewaine's communication. It
contained no reference to our interview of
the preceding day, unless one or two pass-

ing allusions to the prosecution of my legal studies, in playful connexion with my emergence from the ranks of hobbledehoyhood (an event which, in my own estimation, had already taken place) might be so interpreted. Her letter concluded with the following words :—

"As I thought of our uncle, my courage nearly failed me in taking this trip. Should any accident befall him during my absence, I must never hope to forgive myself. Indeed, I almost fear to urge ambition on others, when I behold how completely professional life and professional fame take the part of a second nature."

My poor cousin ! *I* was certainly not that willing steed which the spur is said to be inapplicable to. However, her letter afforded me considerable satisfaction, I might almost say relief. It was an indirect approval of the course which I had taken on the preceding night.

Nevertheless—so arrant a coward is con-

science—I scarcely dared to lift my eyes to
where my uncle was seated across the breakfast-table ; and lost myself in endless conjectures as to whether he knew, or suspected,
aught of my midnight watch. Of the actual
purity of my motives, I entertained some
doubts myself. A desire to be of service to
my uncle, should danger or difficulty demand it, and, more especially, to enter on
my office of fellow-labourer and worker with
my cousin, was, I could honestly avouch,
my primary inducement. But I might not
deny that curiosity—a strong wish to learn
the object of these nocturnal excursions (I
had not, I felt assured, witnessed the first of
them), possessed some little share in the
course which I had pursued. On the whole,
I was not sorry when the meal was concluded,
and the several members separated, each to
his or her usual and peculiar avocations of
the morning.

My epistolary correspondence, however,
was fated to be an unusually long one for
the day. On the arrival of Dan, with the
regular morning's post-bag, I found that it

contained a letter for me from my fellcw-
traveller, Captain Ogleby, and a somewhat
bulky one too. On opening it, some legal
documents, a couple of old newspaper slips,
and the like dropped out. Heedless of these
in the first instance, I had more immediate recourse to the letter which accompanied them.

After reminding me of my promised visit
to Tinnaheely Lodge, and the coming season
big with the fate of partridge and grouse,
the Captain entered upon a subject which at
once arrested all my attention, promising as
it did to clear up a portion of the mystery in
which I now found myself involved—namely,
that referring to my cousin Leslie, and his
enforced absence from his native land. But
I must give the worthy ex-journalist and ex-
Captain's own words; premising, however,
(lest, having just stated, a few pages back,
that I was on the eve of learning the circumstances connected with my cousin Marley's
decease, I might unwittingly disappoint the
reader's expectations) that no explanation of
that event will be found in the following
epistle. I have already laid before him my

reasons for not pushing my inquiries on that point to any extreme extent—and nothing short of that was at all likely to meet response; but with those reasons Captain Ogleby was unacquainted, and it was but natural for him to suppose that I was already in possession of the facts—as, indeed, I was soon to be. His letter, then, will be found to refer mainly to my other cousin Leslie, the son of my present host, Allen Fetherstone —the particulars affecting whom are also essential to the due understanding of my narrative. This premised, the Captain's letter ran as follows, skipping the few introductory lines just alluded to :—

" Do I forfeit all pretensions to the traditionary hospitality of my country by confessing that such has not been my primary motive in sitting down to write to my late fellow-traveller ? Plague take ceremony : come when you will, you know you are at all times welcome.

" The matter more immediately in hand stands thus : I had not parted from you, at the Scalp, above an hour, when I met Lord Killgrove (who, as John Warden, had been a fellow-student of mine at our Irish Alma Mater: I dare not, with my sister's sharp eyes upon me, say how many years ago) driving into town with his daughter—a very charming young lady, by the way. Recognition was mutual, and I was not allowed to proceed until I had promised an early visit to St. Kevin's. Yesterday, I put my gun on my shoulder and strolled across the Yellow Mountain, and had a bit of dinner with him (neither of us forgets when we eked out the meal with a sixpenny snack and a pint of beer). To my surprise—rather, to my pleasure: I knew you were a likely young fellow for it—he recounted what a service a certain young gentleman of our acquaintance had lately done him: by-the-bye, I thought Miss Lucy's eyes—*of course,* you know her name is Lucy—grew brighter as the tale proceeded. 'I wish I could be even with the young fellow,' said his lordship, 'and perhaps I see my way to cry quits.' Now, the way requires explanation, and, between ourselves, some very delicate handling.

"And first, by way of preface, let me apologise for one or two awkward questions which I, in my partial ignorance, put to you at the ' Rose.' I had not then succeeded in connecting your family name with the vague and disjointed rumours which reached me abroad in reference to the events which have deprived the country, I trust for a time only, of your uncle's valuable legal abilities. My head was somewhat clearer by morning, but I judged it the better course to make no further allusion to the subject, nor is there any necessity that I should now enter upon those details, with which you have doubtless by this time made yourself acquainted. Let me rather confine myself to the matter which more immediately presses, viz., the enforced absence of your cousin Leslie, which we both think the present time affords a desirable opportunity to make an effort to bring to a conclusion. As some return for his debt to you, Lord Killgrove professes his desire to move in this matter, should it be placed in

proper training; and I need scarcely tell you
that his position at the Privy Council renders
his assistance of great value. At the same
time, he is but one of many having voices
there, whereby it becomes necessary that his
hands should be further strengthened by putting as fair a case into them as the nature of
the circumstances will permit. He seems in
favour of proceeding by Petition, which he
would back up at the proper time, when it
comes before the Board. But this is a subject for after-consideration; we must first get
up our case. I have no doubt that the
presence of his son would afford much consolation to your uncle under his present
trials; and who knows but a more equable
frame of mind might suggest some mode of
extrication from them also? But now for
the facts which are to be dressed up in the
most presentable form possible. I am, of
course, unaware what conversation has
passed between yourself and your relatives
on this subject; but I readily infer that it
would be painful to your uncle to enter into
those minute details which you may need in

moving in the matter, and that he would prefer you should learn them from other lips. It is with this view—a harmless one at least, if it does not meet your approval—that I have been careful to secure all the leading particulars of the affair—chiefly from Lord Killgrove himself; and these I now enclose. Their sum total, which I may as well here collect for you, runs pretty much as follows.

"I think I told you that the Irish branches of your family had been known in my time, and before it, for their strict loyalty and allegiance to the Crown. The fact is indisputable, and we ought to be able to make something of it ; your uncle's claims should be strong on that head. I was able to assert nothing, however, of the later generation ; and it was as well I did not make the attempt, as after information teaches me. When your cousin Leslie entered the Irish University, a strong revolutionary spirit had already taken hold of a portion of its undergraduates. From all I can hear, I do not believe there was much of the rebel in his constitution; but, in perilous times, the

boundary between Progress and Revolution
is apt to become ill-defined. Not only are
the followers, and more especially the youthful followers, of moral persuasion occasionally
seen hurried on to physical force; but also,
at such periods, the more stable and con-
sistent advocates of the former are suspected
of secret sympathies with the latter. Not,
however, to detain you with a theory, when
time presses—your cousin attached himself
to a band of fellow-collegians, who had
already attracted the notice of the university
authorities by their somewhat imprudent
efforts at oratory and a suspected connexion with the secret movement taking
place outside the walls of the building.

"A few months before that movement
came to a head, a royal Commission held
its sittings in the University, under Lord-
Chancellor Clare (one possessing somewhat
more of the *suaviter in modo* might have
suited the occasion better), to inquire into
these matters; and the expulsion of a number
of students was the result. Robert Emmet,
whose brother had already suffered exile

upon political grounds, was one of the first
whose answers before the members of the
Commission were deemed unsatisfactory;
and the purity of this young man's life, and
his amiable disposition—facts, I believe, uni-
versally acknowledged on all hands—had
begotten so strong a feeling in his favour,
that his rejection was reckoned to have produced an inimical state of mind among his
class fellows toward the Commission, as
evinced by the subsequent responses. Young
Moore, whose poetry is now delighting all
ears (I am just getting through his *Ana-
creon*) was the next called up for questioning,
and, with him, it was all but touch and go.
On rejoining his fellow-collegians in the
body of the Hall, who had been attentive
listeners of Clare's browbeating and the
spirited replies of the youthful bard, he was
received with little short of an ovation; and
your cousin's name was called. Whether
it was in consequence of feelings evoked by
Emmet's rejection and the bold front of
Moore, or that Leslie Featherstone was
really unable to offer a satisfactory explana-

tion, certain it is his replies were judged
wholly inadequate, and public expulsion
was the result. Young Emmet and your
cousin quitted the University walls together;
and acts in connexion with the incipient
Rebellion being traced, shortly after, to
them, sentence of banishment followed. I
believe there would be little difficulty—now
that the confusion and excitement of the
movement itself is past—in bringing home
those acts more particularly to young
Emmet, the action of your relative being
chiefly the promptings of friendship; and,
for this purpose (should such a course be
entered on), I send you the chief documents
bearing upon them. It is a method, however, which I am inclined to think the high
spirit of your cousin would protest against,
and, possibly, overturn by a counter statement, more especially as there is reason to
suppose that the intimacy is still maintained
between himself and Robert Emmet. At all
events, our safest plan would appear to be
to lean mainly on the natural and pardon-
able emotions called into being by the dis-

grace—and, I think we may now assert, the injustice—of a public expulsion, under all the circumstances of the case.

" Consider these matters over with yourself, and, to what extent you think proper, with your relatives. Time is more pressing than might, at first sight, appear to be the case. I cannot disguise from myself—however the Government may pooh-pooh it— that the elements of disaffection are again at work in this country. I have been, of late, thrown among large masses of the peasantry, and their reticence on certain political subjects strongly reminds me of the state of affairs immediately preceding some of our past outbreaks, and convinces me that there is a secret undercurrent at work through the land. If we wait until this arrives at a head, there is little doubt that our matter would come before the Government at an inopportune and unfriendly time. With fire and sword raging through the country, our petition might pray to deaf ears, or receive an unfavourable, and final, answer."

If this epistle did not clear up all that was dark and mysterious about the House of Ravensdale, as previously intimated by me, it at least lifted a portion of the curtain. I could now account for the absence of my cousin Leslie from the country; and I could also interpret the regret with which Miss De Vere spoke of blighted prospects and an interrupted professional career. The letter, it is true, threw no light on the retirement of my uncle from his profession; and I regretted the more that it stopped short of this, inasmuch as, in laying Captain Ogleby's communication before him, which I judged the most proper course to be pursued, I must needs tread on ground, the nature of which I was but imperfectly acquainted with. However, there appeared to be no help for it ; and, provided with the Captain's letter and documents, I left my room in quest of him. Had my cousin Constance been at home, I should have preferred to lay my present difficulty before her, and, at the risk of some pain to her, beseech a clue to the labyrinth on which I was entering ; but

Miss Macklewaine, the only other present inhabitant of Ravensdale House, appeared to me scarcely a desirable person in my emergency, and I chose to come before my uncle unaided, instead.

In truth, I found myself entering on my duties as fellow-worker and adopted brother of Miss De Vere with somewhat of a vengeance, and with very scant breathing-time after my late declaration and its consequence. However, setting aside the sincerity of my resolves on that head, honour and family ties appeared to leave no other course open. Moreover, I could not but regard Lord Killgrove's action in the matter—no very enticing one, where the judicial functions were to be laid aside for those of the advocate, in a cause then anything but popular among his compeers—as a most graceful return for a service which the mere impulses of humanity would have dictated. The least I could do in requital of such attention was to give the present proposal all the prompt and vigorous aid which lay in my power.

Filled with these somewhat conflicting considerations, it was with a near approach to
relief I discovered that I was allowed some
further time for reflection, on learning that
my uncle had left the house soon after the
morning's meal, and was not expected home
until nightfall. Such short absences were
by no means unusual with him; and, in
common with all done by him, were made
without explanation, or previous warning.
My relief, I need scarcely say, had no reference to any change of mind in placing my
uncle in possession of the communication I
had just received. Rather, it was occa-
sioned by this ignorance of much affecting
the position and circumstances of the person
I was about to consult, and by a vague hope
that something might arise in the meantime
to render me better prepared. It was while
considering this view of the matter that old
Martha recurred to my mind. From her, I
might collect much practical information
bearing on the subject of my cousin Leslie's
affairs, and, if she occasionally diverged
into those of my uncle, was there any impro-

priety in my lending an ear to her discourse?
Martha, an old and faithful retainer of the
family, was not to be classed with an ordinary domestic; and, as I had already repeated my visit several times to her cottage,
we were now on pretty near terms of intimacy. In fine, I determined to see Martha
in the course of the day; and, with regard
to the rest, to be guided very much by circumstances, as they might fall out.

My reading, I fear, for that day, did not
add much to my stores of legal knowledge.
Martha was not likely to be in a confidential
— possibly, an amiable — frame of mind
during the bustle of the noon-day, and our
interview was further liable to interruption
from the intrusion of neighbours. I had set
apart, therefore, the shades of evening for
my visit—and it was not without relief that
I, at length, saw their approach. Our
dinner-table had presented a comparatively
dreary waste, and not even the friendly
assistance of Dan was able to impart liveli-
ness to the conversation which I and Miss
Macklewaine endeavoured to maintain over

it. On the occasions of a day's absence from home, my uncle usually returned at a late hour, and then retired to his room; from which he did not issue until the following morning. I could not call to mind any instance in which his seclusion, at such periods, had been broken in on; and it was a question with me whether my present business with him was of so urgent a nature as to absolve me in breaking through what appeared to me to be an understood rule of the house. After some reflection with myself, I decided in the negative; and determined to await the morning for my interview with him.

This decided, I sat down to acknowledge the receipt of Captain Ogleby's letter— thanking him for his communication, informing him of the temporary absence of my uncle from home, and of my intention of placing the matter before him on the following morning. At the present juncture, it was, I feared, impossible for me to leave Ravensdale House; but I hoped to have a day at the partridges before the season terminated.

By the time I had sealed my letter and deposited it in the post-bag on the hall-table, I was surprised to find that the hours had slipped by more hastily than I had ventured to hope ; and not only had the shades of evening, but even nightfall itself, made its appearance, as I issued from the house.

A bright and warm day had been succeeded by a sultry, lowering evening. Black clouds sailed slowly into the hitherto blue sky, and took up their positions in dense packed masses. Large drops of rain pattered at intervals among the superabundant foliage ; and all the signs of a coming summer thunderstorm became visible around. Indeed, I had not proceeded far when the distant *crepitus* informed me that Heaven's artillery was already getting into preparation; and, every now and again, a stray flash of lightning illumined the thickly-overshadowed path which led to the cottage.

" Hurry in, Masther Frank, out of the rain," was the exclamation of Martha, as, standing at her door, in apparent contemplation of the contending elements, she perceived my approach.

Deeming it best to be perfectly above-board with the old lady, I gave her a rapid sketch of the unexpected communication I had received from Captain Ogleby,—explaining, as reasons for my ignorance of past family matters, my absence from Ireland, and, for several years, from the paternal roof.

" Dear knows," was the reply of Martha, " it would do my old heart good to see the boy back in his father's house, where he ought to be. And why wouldn't he stand up for his country, if he saw her badly used? —anyhow, there's many of his way of thinking."

Unwilling to bring on a political discussion, with matters more pressing in hand, I suggested (such appearing to me to be my most powerful line of argument with the old retainer) the traditionary loyalty of the family.

" Ay ; the Featherstones were ever for king and country—see the reward they met."

Finding it improbable that I should be able to hold my own on this topic, I now sought to divert the patriotic mind of Martha to the more immediate object of my visit—with somewhat better effect.

" True for you, Masther Frank," was her remark, in reply to an attempt of mine in this direction, " there's been sorrow and throuble enough already. It's like * of you to think of the poor exile. I only hope the Masther will agree to it."

" Agree ! Martha. Surely my uncle would place no impediment in the way of his son's return ? "

" I dunna—he's not the man he was. No one knows what's in his mind now."

" Yet, Martha, you must have some reason for speaking as you do. Surely his loyalty would not go to the lengths of rendering him more inexorable than the laws which his son has offended ! "

" No ; I have heard him talk of the boy's act as a freak of youth. But speak to himself, Masther Frank—speak to himself.

* Like the natural disposition of your family.

Maybe he'll let out his mind to you. Time
was when he'd tell ould Martha whatever
troubled him."

"These matters," I resumed—giving expression, indeed, to the thoughts which suggested themselves to my mind, rather than
addressing Martha—"these matters occurred prior to the event which caused my
uncle to abandon his profession?"

"Thrue, Masther Frank—the Masther
was cheerful enough for many a day after,
and told us he'd have his son back with him
as soon as the country was settled."

"I *will* speak to my uncle, Martha—of
course it is my intention to lay this whole
matter before him in the morning. But the
doubts you now seem to throw upon his
willingness to co-operate with us, take me
wholly by surprise—and, insufficiently acquainted with the circumstances which
affect him, I possess few means of com-
bating them."

Under a national suavity—which has long
obtained for itself the title of "blarney"—
the Irish peasant conceals a very consider-

able portion of cunning—as a protection, doubtless, against any risks which over-politeness might lead into. I now saw that Martha—spite of her compliments and pro-testations—was revolving in her own mind to what extent I might be taken with safety into the domestic confidence, and whether my visit and the conversation which had arisen out of it were not all a clever *ruse* on my part to arrive at the family history. Apparently, the matter was eventually de-cided in my favour—though, whether in consideration of the disinterestedness of my motives, or the powerful inducement of having a perfectly new ear to tell her tale to, I had no means of judging.

" Biddy, alanna" (this was addressed to a young girl, a granddaughter of hers, who lived with her), " say your prayers, astore, and go to bed—it's in your second sleep you ought to be by this time."

And as the child, in obedience to the command, retired within the inner room, the dame added to me—

" Them children, Masther Frank, have

sharp ears, and, if Biddy overheard us, it's little she'd sleep to-night."

Having so far cleared the course, Martha re-arranged the burning embers on the hearth, drew forth her short pipe, and, having fully ignited it by a few preliminary whiffs, placed her elbows on her knees, and, bending over the hearth in the true Irish crone fashion, commenced the strange tale which the reader will find in the following chapter.

END OF VOL. I.

THE

MISTRESS OF LANGDALE HALL:

A ROMANCE OF THE WEST RIDING.

By ROSA M. KETTLE,

Author of ' Smugglers and Foresters,' etc.

WITH FRONTISPIECE AND VIGNETTE BY P. SKELTON.

Price 4s., Post Free.

"It is interesting and very pleasantly written ; and for the sake of both author and publisher, we cordially wish it the reception it deserves."—*Saturday Review.*

"The most careful mother need not hesitate to place it at once in the hands of the most unsophisticated daughter. As regards the publisher, we can honestly say that the type is clear and the book well got up in every way."—*Athenæum.*

"There is a naturalness in this novel, published in accordance with Mr. Tinsley's very wholesome one-volumed system, which will attract many quiet readers. We will just express our satisfaction at the portable and readable size of the book."—*Spectator.*

"'The Mistress of Langdale Hall' is a bright and attractive story, which can be read from beginning to end with pleasure."— *Daily News.*

"The story itself is really well told, and some of the characters are delineated with great vividness and force. The tone of the book is high. The writer shows considerable mastery of her art."— *Nonconformist.*

"The book is a model of what a cheap novel should be."—*Publishers' Circular.*

"A circular from the publisher precedes the opening of the novel, wherein the existing conditions of novel-publishing are concisely set forth. It is ably and smartly written, and forms by no means the least interesting portion of the contents of the volume. We strongly recommend its perusal to novel readers generally."—*Welshman.*

SAMUEL TINSLEY, Southampton Street, Strand.